ALL THE LITTLE MOMENTS

SAVANNAH REED

5 PRINCE PUBLISHING
5PRINCEBOOKS.COM

Published by:

5 Prince Publishing and Books, LLC

DBA 5 Prince Publishing

PO Box 865

Arvada, Colorado 80001

This is a work of fiction. Names, characters, places, and incidents are the product of the author's imagination or are used fictitiously. Any resemblance to actual persons, living or dead, events, or locales is entirely coincidental.

Digital ISBN: 978-1-63112-410-5

Print ISBN: 978-1-63112-411-2

Cover design by Marianne Nowicki

First Edition F07172025

For more information about this title, visit: www.5princebooks.com

Mom & Dad
Thanks for telling me I should be an English major.
This one's for you.

ACKNOWLEDGMENTS

Everyone says that writing a book is hard, and boy are they right! This has been an experience unlike any other, but I'm incredibly proud of myself for pushing through the challenges and bringing my very first book to life. It all started in late 2020, at a time when I, like many others, was feeling lost. My dad came to me with an idea, and I decided to start writing a book with him. I didn't realize this decision would set in motion something much larger than I could have imagined. A few months later, while I was deep in the writing process, I had this dream. I woke up the next morning and immediately started writing it all down, knowing this story had to be told. And, well, that's how this book was born. Little did I know what a journey Chase, Tatum, and Emma would take me on. It's hard to believe it's over, but this book will always have a piece of my heart. So, I want to thank you, my wonderful readers, for picking up this book and taking this journey with me. I can't express how much this means to me.

First and foremost, I want to thank my parents. John and Pam Kacpura. Thank you for everything you've done for me—I wouldn't be where I am if it wasn't for you two. Thank you for not only putting me through college, but also encouraging me to major in English because of my love for reading and writing. Dad, thank you for paving the way with the creative spark you started back in 2020 when you came to me with this idea and said, "Hey, this could be a cool book!" While I may have veered off and written a completely different book (oops!), I promise our book is coming. Mom, the grammar queen, thank you for understanding why I couldn't share this book with you until it was finished. (Thank you, thank you, thank you for everything). I don't know how to repay you, but I hope this dedication is a meaningful start!

I want to give a heartfelt thank you to my amazing publisher, Bernadette Marie, and everyone at 5 Prince Publishing for taking a chance on me. Bernadette, you've turned my dream into a reality, and I can't begin to express how truly grateful I am. A huge thank you to Courtney Davis for reading my pitch and seeing the potential in this story from the start. And of course, I'm deeply thankful to my wonderful editor, Cate Byers. Thank you for helping me find my footing in the world of edits and for telling me when things were or weren't working (in the kindest way possible), and for all your hard work in helping me bring this book to life.

To my Charleston girls – you know who you are. A million thanks for being my unwavering moral support, for lifting me up through every moment of self-doubt, and sending me a care package when I was feeling down. Thank you for listening to my endless snapchats asking you all if what I wrote sounds good or not. Thank you to Madalaine Doran, for reading this book and being my built-in therapist at times (no, seriously, she really is a therapist). And to Caroline Quinney, for being my biggest cheerleader, for standing by my side since '98, for reading my book (yes, I'll get it on audiobook for you—eventually), and for being the inspiration behind Courtney's character. I don't know where I'd be without every one of you. I love you all.

Thank you to all my wonderful friends in Chattanooga—the Waters, Sullivans, Rose-Rodriguezes, Whittakers, McClures, Mattsons, and Wuerfels. I love you all dearly and I appreciate each one of you. You've all made such an impact on my life and I'm lucky to have an amazing group of friends like you all. Thank you for always checking in and asking, "How's the book coming?" and for patiently answering all my baby questions because I didn't have a clue. Your support means more to me than you'll ever know.

Thank you to Brittany Duncan, for being my first editor when I came to you with this baby manuscript, uncertain and unsure of what I was doing. You believed in me from the start and gave me the confidence to keep going. Because of you, this story was made possible and became something I'm truly proud of.

My book club girls! Ciscily Stewart, Maci Culver, Kat Allen, Ellen Boone (Ms. Boone!), Julie Stoll, Kiyoko Puca-Andrews, Laura Holland—and to the other girls who haven't had the opportunity to read it yet—words can't express how grateful I am for each of you. The encouragement and support you have so selflessly showed me has been a constant source of strength throughout this journey. I'm beyond lucky to be surrounded by such an inspiring group of women. I love you all, girly pops. A special thank you to Ciscily, whose frequent "when can I read it?" finally gave me the courage to share this story with others. And for somehow convincing me to let everyone read it as our book of the month (not scary at all …).

And now, the most important thank you of all: to my incredible husband, Bradford Dixon. This book quite literally wouldn't have been possible without you. I have relied so much on your strength, generosity, and patience during this long process of writing. Thank you for always believing I could do this even when I didn't. Thank you for encouraging me through all my moments of self-doubt and crying happy tears with me when I found out this book was getting published. Thank you for reading my manuscript not once, but twice, with all its flaws and giving me feedback on it (even though I couldn't stand when you would highlight and write down notes right in front of me— "Uh, do you know how to spell wrinkled?"). I know how much you hate reading, and yet you took your time to read it whenever I asked, so thank you. Thank you for everything you've done to fulfill this dream of mine, I'm beyond grateful to have you by my side. I love you endlessly.

To my family, friends, and everyone else who believed in me along the way and made me feel like I could truly be an author—this book exists because of you. I wouldn't be here today, holding this book in my hands, if it wasn't for everyone's unwavering support. And to those I haven't mentioned by name, please know that I appreciate you and I love you. Thank you, from the bottom of my heart.

ALL THE LITTLE MOMENTS

CHAPTER 1

I stare at my mother incredulously, my mouth hanging open like a fish out of water, gasping for air. It's like I'm hearing the words without actually comprehending them. Because what she's saying can't possibly be real.

"What do you mean?" I demand.

"Look, honey," my mother says with an exasperated sigh, "it will be the best for everyone in the long run." Her short, honey-blonde hair, so much like my own, sways back and forth as she lightly shakes her head. The multiple gold bracelets on her wrist jingle together as she reaches up to tuck a few strands of hair back into place. I don't think I've ever seen my mother not looking put together. I swear she wakes up extra early to do her hair and makeup that gives her the effortlessness of the 'just woke up' look that many influencers have. I'm barely able to hold back my snort at that thought; now is definitely not the right time to think about that. Plus, I highly doubt my mother would find it as funny as I do.

I return to the conversation at hand. "Right, it will be best for you and your reputation but not for me and my child. What do you think that will do to a kid?"

"Which is precisely why we are going through the court system. This will never be brought up again, nor will the child know any differently." She looks at me with a penetrating glare. I know that look. It isn't just a look of disappointment though; no, I've received those stares all my life. It's more like a look of regret —regret that I'm not the perfect child they wanted. *Well too bad.* I will always be their daughter who got pregnant in high school, whether they like it or not. I narrow my eyes back at her.

It's not like I got pregnant on purpose, of course. I never really even had a rebellious phase. Most of the kids at my school have done things much worse, though nothing as permanent as having a child, I suppose. Even if they did, their parents would have covered it up before anyone knew what to gossip about. Which is exactly what my parents did. Because when you grow up in a small Connecticut town where money flows faster than champagne, you tend to have the mindset that rules don't apply to you. I learned early on that you could solve just about anything with a little money or blackmail.

I grew up trying to be the perfect child; I really did. I followed their rules, went to their parties, and mingled with their friends at the club. I went to all the same after-school activities and took the same lessons as the girls in my grade did. A part of me thinks they wanted me to be perfect to compensate for their own insecurities. My parents were high school sweethearts who got married their junior year of college. My mom had constantly made it known that she wanted to be a young stay-at-home mom with a whole brood of kids. So, when they immediately tried— and failed—to get pregnant, those dreams of having a house full of children running around flew out the window. They threw their money at anything and everything that might help them conceive a baby. Finally, after years and years of watching their friends around them having kids, they had me.

I was their rainbow baby that would carry on the Rothchild legacy. They prepared me to do everything a classy socialite is expected to do. I took private lessons, attended a private school, and even went to their precious private parties. Private, private, private; God, I hate that word. For a town that has the word private in almost everything, nothing about your life remained a secret here. Although, I guess I was somehow the exception. The news of my pregnancy was kept so tight-lipped that no one outside of mine or Adam's family knew about it. Honestly, if I hadn't watched my stomach swell for nine months and then given birth, I wouldn't have even known I had a child. That's how secretive everything was. I've learned that's what happens when you have an obscene amount of money; if there's a problem, money can fix it.

The feel of paper sliding into my hands brings me back to the present. I'm speechless as I stare down at the thick stack of papers splayed out in my lap. My fingers clutch the crisp, smooth sheets, trembling slightly as I read the first few words. The only thing that stands out to me is the one word I still can't believe: adoption. These are adoption papers my mother has just handed me. There's no way this can be happening. I thought they accepted this. I glare up at my mom in disbelief.

"You can't be serious."

"Honey," my mother replies in her sickly-sweet voice. "This is for the best, I promise." My hands curl into fists, creating creases on the smooth surface of the papers. She knows how much I hate it when she calls me honey, acting like a loving mother.

"It's bullshit!" I yell.

"Tatum Marie! Watch your language," she scolds, but I ignore her reprimand, trying hard not to roll my eyes.

"You honestly think that my boyfriend's parents raising my baby is for the best?" Letting go of the now crinkled paper, I swipe a hand through my hair. "This is why you've acted like everything is fine, isn't it? How long have you been planning this?" I demand to know.

She glances up at me, her fingers paused over her phone I

didn't even notice she had out, as if whatever email or text she's sending is more important than this conversation. She sighs, locking her phone and placing it down in her lap. "Claire came up with the idea shortly after you told us you were pregnant. We all agreed that this was the best solution, rather than giving the baby to some random strangers. After all, this baby comes from two powerful families. What better way for it to grow up than in a house with loving parents?" She waves me away, a satisfied glint in her eye that shows me just how proud she is of this solution.

This time I can't hold back my eye roll. "And what makes you think I'd give her up? And she already has two *loving parents* with Adam and me!" I yell the last part, my face heating in anger with each word. How dare she? Then something she said makes me pause. "Wait, when you say we ... does Adam know about this?" I ask, praying she won't say the very thing that will make this worse than it is.

Adam Livingston. My beacon of light throughout my childhood, my best friend, my first love, and the father of my baby. We grew up together, never knowing a time when we didn't live next door to each other. He's the youngest in his family, the same age as me, with four older sisters. We often joked about how I was the rainbow baby, while he was the accidental one. With four sisters you'd think he'd want more testosterone in his life, but somehow, we became inseparable. He understood and easily adapted to the life we had, helping me to navigate it.

As the years went by and we got older, he became the boy I fell in love with. The way he styled his bright blond hair to perfection and how he would smile at me as though I was the greatest thing to walk the earth. I felt safe with him, like he was my protector. Like he saw all the jagged parts of me and wanted to make me whole again. I had dreams of us exploring the world together, creating a beautiful life for ourselves. I just never realized how one accident would lead us to this path we are on now.

My mother's voice draws me back. "Of course he does, honey," she reveals, sending me a look that would probably appear sympathetic if it wasn't for the slight smirk forming on her lips. "His father is good friends with the dean at Yale, as you know, and there has been talk of him getting an early acceptance. You know it's always been his dream to attend Yale, but he can't very well do that with a baby, now can he?"

Once again, I find myself speechless, my eyes blinking comically in disbelief at her. Is that all they can think about—his future? As if having a child means he can't go to college. What about our future together, our daughter's future? The trajectory of her life hangs in the balance of this decision that my mother, and apparently Adam, has forced me into. Sure, this isn't as conventional as I thought it would be, but I always pictured Adam and I getting married and starting a family. This has just sped up that process a little bit. Yet, all this time, he knew. He knew about our parents' ploy to give our baby up without my knowledge, and he was *okay* with it.

"And you just expect me to be okay with his parents raising her? With Adam still living in that house and me here, right next door, spending our senior year like nothing happened?"

"I really don't understand why you are fighting with me on this. It works out for everybody. The Livingstons can have another child—I think they've done fairly well with the five they already have—and now you and Adam can have a real shot at a future together. You two can finish up your senior year and go off to college. Then, you can join a sorority and have some fun before settling down. We hid your pregnancy so well that no one will ever know about this. They'll all just think that the Livingstons adopted a new baby like the wonderful people they are." She waves her hand dismissively in the air. "It's all sorted out and everyone is on board with the idea. You just need to accept that this is happening. Okay?"

I start shaking my head before she has even finished speaking, swallowing the rock in my throat. "And what if I don't agree to this?"

My heart sinks at her dazzling smile, the one that looks like the cat that got the cream. I know exactly what that smile means. "Well, as you're still a minor, I believe you don't *actually* have a say in the matter. This was more of a courtesy warning for you, and honestly, Tatum, I was hoping you'd be more appreciative of us doing you this favor. But seeing you're as stubborn as always, we'll be going ahead with the legal work next week. The papers are already drawn up, the only thing left to do is sign them," she levels me with a stern glare, "and you *will* sign them."

With that final bomb dropped on me, she stands from my bed, smoothing out the invisible wrinkles on her dress. Without waiting for me to reply she nods and says, "Glad we had this talk. Now, we have your father's business dinner tonight and will be out late. Maria will fix you something to eat." And just like that, I'm dismissed.

I stare after her retreating figure and watch as she brings her phone to her ear, acting as if she didn't just turn my world upside down. I slowly sink back down onto my bed, tears welling in my eyes. I spot my phone on the bedside table and grab it. I scroll until I find his name, but my hand stills, hovering over the call button. I keep thinking back to the fact that Adam knew. He knew this whole time and led me to believe he was on my side. He let me think that I could trust him, and I believed every lie he spewed. The hope that had bloomed in my mind and heart, images of us being a happy family, blow up like smoke in my face until they're just ashes on the ground. With a frustrated sigh, I lock my phone and slam it on my bed. This can't be happening. How dare they try to take away my baby? I refuse to let them do this and I will fight tooth and nail to make sure Emma stays with me.

An hour later, after I've fed Emma and have been mind-numbingly scrolling through social media, I decide I can't take it anymore. I go to my contacts and find his name, hitting the call button before I chicken out again. My hands shake as I press the phone to my ear and I take a deep, calming breath, trying not to let my nerves get the better of me. As I listen to it ring, I wonder if maybe my mother lied about the whole thing. What if she was just trying to pit us against each other? What if Adam really has no idea about any of this? Will he be just as upset as me? My mind is racing with so many possibilities that I almost miss the distinct *click* of him answering the phone.

"Tatum."

The cold tone I hear on the other end has my forehead creasing. I take the phone away from my ear and stare down at it, making sure I called the right person. But there it is, in bold letters at the top of the screen, Adam's name with a red heart next to it.

"Adam," I hesitantly start, "what's going on?"

His exasperated sigh echoes down the line. "I'm assuming your mother told you the plan." It isn't a question, and it only confirms everything I hoped wasn't true.

"Yes, she told me," I growl, my anger from when my mother first told me returning. "And how can you think that I'd be even remotely okay with this? I thought we would get through this together. That's what you told me. Why would you agree to something like this?" My voice has steadily been rising and by the time I'm finished I'm yelling. I take a deep breath, my chest heaving, and I rub my hand over it to try and relieve some of the pressure that's been building.

"Tay." He says it so softly I barely hear him at first.

My heart stutters in my chest; he knows that's my weak spot.

One day, back when we were kids, he had found me quietly crying in my backyard. He rushed over and threw his arms around me, asking why I was so upset. I told him I was sad that I didn't have a cool nickname like some of the other girls in my class. How Betty Johnson, whose real name was Bethany, would snicker at me and tell me everyone liked her more and that's why they called her Betty. Although, I'm pretty sure it was her parents who first started calling her Betty. I remember the resolve on his face as he looked at me and proudly stated, *"Of course you have a nickname. Hmm, let me think. How about Tay? Just forget about the 'tum' part. I can call you Tay from now on, if you'd like?"* He had looked over at me with those sparkling emerald eyes and I swore my heart was about to leap out of my chest. It seemed inconsequential at the time, a silly little ploy to make me feel better, but it meant the world to me.

"Tay," he repeats, louder this time. I realize I never answered him, too busy getting swept up in the memory.

"Don't. Don't say that like you're not ripping my heart out and destroying our future," I hiss.

"I'm protecting our future!" he yells. It's so sudden, so unlike him, that I'm stunned speechless for a second time today. I blink, trying to think of something to say, but no words seem to come out. He takes my silence as an invitation to keep talking, his voice much softer this time. "Our lives are ruined, Tay. I know you're not ready to be a parent; I'm sure as hell not. But this way we can have it all. We can go to college together just like we've planned and then, once we graduate and get married, we can seriously talk about having kids. It'll be perfect, Tay, just like you've always wanted."

I feel the tears start to well up in my eyes. I know exactly what he's talking about; it's something I've fallen asleep to—dreaming about what our future would look like. "But we already have a kid. And while we're out there living our own lives, she'll grow up without us. I don't want that, Adam. I want her."

"Well, I don't." His cold tone breaking my heart even more than I thought it could. How can he talk so callously about his own child? He takes a deep breath and regains his composure. "It's for the best, I promise. You'll thank me for this later, once you see how right I am. You're just not thinking clearly right now, and that's okay. But I don't want to risk our future for this."

I'm already shaking my head before he finishes speaking, my hand flying to my mouth to hold back the sobs that I desperately want to let free. I can't lose myself right now, not yet. Gone are his soft attempts to persuade me, like trying to tame a wild animal; instead, replaced with a version sounding so completely unattached that I feel the cracks forming around my heart.

"Just sign the papers so we can finally put this mess behind us and move on with our lives. It'll be you and me against the world again." Without waiting for my response, if I could even come up with one, he mumbles a low *talk to you later* before hanging up. I swallow the lump in my throat as I realize that, for the second time today, I'm being dismissed. It stings more than it did the first time. I expected it from my mother—I'm used to it, actually —but with Adam it feels so much worse. Coming from the boy who had my back, who swore to always protect me, hurts like nothing I've ever felt before.

I finally allow the dam to burst free, feeling the hot tears running down my cheeks. I'm fighting between feeling overwhelming sadness and a fiery outrage. I curl up in a ball on my bed, my phone clutched tightly in my hands, as my mind replays all the events of today over and over again. Eventually, though, the tears dry up and I turn my head to stare up at the ceiling. I can still faintly make out the outline of the glow in the dark stars I know are up there. My nanny at the time, Camilla, put those up there for me. I was eight and afraid of the dark, terrified to go to sleep without the nightlight my mother had just taken away from me. She claimed that I was too old to need it anymore. So, that first night without it, I stared into the dark abyss frozen in fear, not getting a wink of sleep. The next day I told Camilla about it, and she instantly found a solution. She placed those stars on the ceiling above my bed. *Our little secret*, she said. She told me that whenever I was afraid to fall asleep at night, all I had to do was look up and remember that I was safe because the stars would always protect me. My mother never found out about it, but Camilla was fired a few months later. I'm not sure why, but I kept the stars up there, constantly reminding me of her.

I feel a smile tug at my lips from the memory. I sigh and sit up, knowing that I can't wallow in a spiral of despair any longer, and glance at the time on my phone. It's already mid-afternoon, and Emma will probably wake up from her nap soon. I know I should do something, anything, but I feel like I'm drifting underwater with the tides turned against me. How can I protect Emma? Can I live with myself watching her grow up from afar? When did Adam become this cruel to me?

My thoughts continue their turmoil in my head when I feel a buzz in my palm. I look down and see Courtney's name on the screen, along with a picture of her making a goofy face that she insisted I set as her contact picture. I smile and answer it instinctively, almost immediately regretting my decision because there's no way she won't know something's up. That girl is like a magnet for drama.

"Hey," I say, hoping I sound somewhat normal.

"Girl, have you heard?" I panic for a second, thinking she somehow found out about my situation, but she continues, completely oblivious to my internal freakout. "Emily found out that Brad is apparently cheating on her with Josie, which they both deny, but like, come on, we all know he is, and went full nuclear on them when she saw them together at *Twisted Cones* yesterday. I'm talking chocolate ice cream *everywhere*. It was amazing. Senior year is going to be a blast," she sighs wistfully.

Brad and Emily are—*were*, I guess—the most popular couple at our school. I know Adam desperately wanted that title for us, but I never cared about that stuff. When we would hang out with that group, it was all about one-upping each other with who had the better vacation house or what new expensive gift daddy dearest got them this time. Courtney and I never really got along with them, but Adam insisted on dragging me to all their parties. I can't help but wonder if that's why Adam's pushing this adoption so much. If he thinks we'll become the new "it couple" now that they've been dethroned.

I know Courtney's waiting for me to reply, but all I can manage is, "Oh wow."

"I know, right? It was epic." I hear what sounds like her plopping down on her bed. "So, how's my little goddaughter doing?"

"Good. She's napping right now." I smile and look towards the door. Like if I look hard enough, I can see her sleeping in her crib.

"Ugh," she groans. "She is *so* freaking cute I just want to squish her little cheeks. FaceTime is just not enough."

A watery smile takes over my face. Courtney has been one of my biggest supporters, even if it was in secret. "I wish you could see her too, but you know my mother would kill me if she ever found out that you know about Emma."

I can just feel the eye roll from here. "Yeah, right. You know that evil wench doesn't scare me."

"Well, she should. Especially after what happened today."

"What the hell happened today?" she asks, suddenly alert.

I can't stop the sob that escapes me. I would think that after all the crying I've already done, there wouldn't be anything left, yet the tears flow freely. Courtney's been exactly what I needed in a friend, much to my mother's disdain. She regularly voiced her disapproval of our friendship, so, over the years, we learned how to hide it, which only seemed to make our bond grow stronger. I met Courtney on the first day of middle school, when she defended me against Will Newell, a cruel boy who liked to bully me. Courtney overheard him being mean and punched him in the face. When I swung my shocked gaze over to her, she simply shrugged and stated *jerks get what they deserve.* I was stunned at first, but I also couldn't help being drawn to her enigmatic personality. She was different from all the other kids I had grown up with, so I decided to sit with her during detention later that afternoon and she's been my best friend ever since.

Once I finally calm down enough, I explain everything that happened. I tell her about the talk with my mother, with Adam, and their ridiculous plans for the adoption.

"I'm sorry, they're doing what?!" Courtney screeches down the line once I've finished telling her everything. I pull the phone away from my ear for a second, listening to her incoherent rambling on the other end. "What kind of sick, twisted little shits do they think they are? I'd like to show them how small-minded their little fish brains actually are. *Please* tell me you went off on them."

Despite everything else going on, I can't help but chuckle at that. Sometimes her long-winded rants make absolutely no sense, but I still love her for them. "You know I didn't," I say with a sigh.

"Yeah, I know," she says, sounding resigned, "but I wish you did. God, I can imagine it now. Your mother wouldn't know what hit her."

"Oh yeah. Grab your popcorn for a front row seat at what a shit show my life has become," I say sarcastically.

She sighs. "Your life isn't a shit show, you were just dealt some pretty shitty cards. But look, I'm here for you and we'll work something out. This isn't the end of the road; I promise you that."

"Thanks Court. You have no idea how much I needed to hear that," I say with my first real smile today.

"I've got your back, babe. Forever and always."

I swipe a hand across my cheek, removing the leftover tears that stain them. "I just can't believe that Adam's okay with this and everything he said to me. He's usually on my side, and yeah, this is a big adjustment, but I thought I could at least count on him."

"Doesn't surprise me," she murmurs softly.

I sit up straighter. "What do you mean?" I ask. I hear her deep sigh through the phone, like she really doesn't want to admit anything, but I know there's no going back now. "Courtney," I press.

She groans. "I never wanted to say anything because you two were together all the time, and you looked at him with hearts in your eyes, but that dude is a grade-A asshole."

"What?" I ask in disbelief.

"I know you don't want to hear that, Tatum, but it's true. He treats everyone around him like garbage while acting like he's God's gift to them. It's ridiculous."

My brain is spinning at the bomb she just dropped on me. I know Adam is popular, and yeah, okay, sometimes acts better than others, but so do most of the kids at our school. It's not like you don't know what you're signing up for. Tremont Academy produces the best of the best, and with that comes a ruthlessness that all families in this town have. Adam helped me understand that, but I always thought he never truly bought into any of it. Maybe Courtney's right; I was so blinded by him that I never bothered to question anything he said or did.

"I never realized that," I mumble numbly. There's been so much information dropped on me today that my brain can barely comprehend it.

"Of course you didn't. And I never wanted to say anything because you seemed so happy. I mean, even when you found out you were pregnant, you were scared but happy. I just wanted to make sure you stayed that way. Lord knows with your home life you need a little happiness." She's not wrong. I loved the affection and attention Adam gave me and when I saw that positive plus sign on the test, I thought it would only grow.

"Yeah, well, look where that got me," I tell her ironically. "I mean, seriously, what am I supposed to do now? Obviously, I can't count on anyone anymore, and I have, like, a week to figure out how to fix this because losing my baby isn't an option. I can't let that happen, Court, I just can't."

"You can count on me," she says supportively. Then with a newfound confidence, she tells me, "and you won't. We'll figure a way out of this, I promise. I've gotten myself out of so many different problems they should call me Houdini." I snort, and both of us start cracking up at her lame attempt at a joke.

Once our laughter fades, a somberness descends over the phone. I clear my throat and tell her earnestly, "Thank you. I really don't know where I'd be without you. You're the best."

In true Courtney fashion, she replies, "I know I am."

I shake my head. "Brat."

"Yeah, but you love me."

"You know I do."

"Get some rest, take care of that precious angel baby, and I'll call you tomorrow with a plan."

"Okay, thank you again."

She pauses for a minute before saying, "Hey, Tatum."

"Yeah?"

"Don't give up hope yet, okay?"

"I won't. Promise." I hang up the phone and I'm grateful that, for once, I'm not the one being silenced by others.

I spend the rest of the evening going through my normal routine of getting Emma ready for bed and when I put her in her crib, I take a little extra time to stare at her beautiful face. Emma brings me more happiness than I ever thought possible. I turn on her white noise machine and glance around the makeshift nursery, suddenly realizing how naïve I've been. There's barely anything in her room. Only her crib and a changing table take up the space. There's no rocking chair for me to sit with her, no books on a shelf to read to her, and no pink-painted walls. Even her crib is just a portable one that my mother insisted I get because Emma wouldn't need it for very long. I should've seen the signs. Like how my mother convinced me that we didn't need to renovate the bedroom into a full nursery right away. I see it for what it is now. It's a temporary solution to appease me. A way to lure me into a false sense of security before pulling the rug out from under me. I look down at Emma's sleeping form and remind myself that she's here right now and I'll do everything in my power to make sure she stays with me. I grab the baby monitor and head back to my room across the hall, praying that Courtney comes up with some sort of solution.

CHAPTER 2

I wake up the following morning with a pounding headache and a growling stomach. I groan with the realization that I never made it downstairs last night to get any dinner. I swipe my hands over my face and grab my phone from the nightstand. The bright light from it makes me squint for a minute before my eyes adjust. With the amount of crying I did last night, I wouldn't be surprised if my eyes were red and puffy. I don't have any new notifications, not that I thought I would, but it's when I check the time that I start to panic. Emma usually wakes me up through the monitor around seven, but it's almost eight now, and I haven't heard a peep from her. I throw off the covers as quickly as I can and make a beeline for her room. Images of my mother and Adam taking her away from me with evil smiles and malicious intentions not only plagued my dreams but now my reality. Surely, they wouldn't have taken her already, would they? I would've woken up if I heard them, wouldn't I?

The breath whooshes out of my lungs as soon as I open the door because there she is, still asleep in her crib with her white noise machine going. I sag against the door frame and let out a sob I didn't realize had built up inside me. The very thought of her being taken from me in the middle of the night makes me sick. I take a deep breath and slowly back out of the room, closing the door softly. I might as well get a bottle ready for her while she's sleeping, so I grab her monitor from my room and head downstairs. There's not a soul in the kitchen when I get there; not even a hint that Maria, our cook, was here to make breakfast. I know she was, though, from the dish in the fridge covered in plastic wrap. I peer down at it and crinkle my nose when I see that it's some tomato frittata concoction. I close the door and grab a banana from the counter; my stomach probably can't handle anything more than that anyway with how much it's been churning. I walk over to the cupboard that has a few of Emma's bottles in it and grab one. I take out the bin of formula next to it and get to work making her a bottle.

It makes me think back to when my mother told me it was best to switch over to formula instead of continuing to breastfeed, that it would make it easier for when I went back to school. I had gotten so excited about going back to school that I never bothered to question it. I had just assumed she meant it would be easier for the nanny we would hire to watch Emma while I wasn't here. Again, that's what I get for assuming and trusting her. Because what she really meant was that when Adam's parents adopted Emma, she would already be on formula and wouldn't have to rely on me anymore. I feel completely blindsided as a fiery rage starts burning inside me at how they think they could do this to me. Grabbing my things off the counter with more force than intended, I go upstairs and drop them off in my room before going across the hall to wake Emma.

"Hi, my sweet little angel," I say as she lets out a big yawn, showing off her gummy little mouth. Her eyes blink up at me and I smile down at her.

After quickly changing her diaper, I walk back to my room with her cradled in my arms. I settle us on the bed and bring the bottle to Emma's mouth, watching as she latches onto it and starts drinking. Her little eyes stare up at me, and I use my index finger that's holding the bottle to run it over her soft cheek. I take in all the different features of her face, trying to pinpoint what she inherited from me or from Adam. Without realizing it, the tears break free and silently fall down my face. I want to be strong, but just the thought of her living right next door and not being able to feed her, hold her, go to her when she cries, and look into her eyes that show nothing but love and trust, breaks my heart. Add in the fact that Adam would go along with it, prepared to spend his senior year pretending that his own daughter is his new baby sister. I hold back the sob that wants to escape, hating that these thoughts consume me, and take a deep breath. Even though it feels impossible, there has to be a way out of this.

Once Emma finishes her bottle, I grab one of the bib cloths I have stashed in my nightstand. I gently shift her until she rests against my shoulder and pat her back, starting the burping process. About halfway through I hear my phone buzz, and I look around to find it, trying not to jostle Emma too much. I find it stuffed under the pile of pillows on my bed and pick it up one-handed, still cradling Emma over my shoulder. Seeing Courtney's name flash across the screen, I choose to ignore it for the moment, knowing it won't be a short conversation. Standing up, I walk over to Emma's bassinet I still have in my room. I lay Emma down in it before going over to the oversized chair next to it and get situated, tucking my feet under me. I go to call Courtney back, but before I can even unlock my phone, my screen lights up with her name again. Shaking my head I swipe to answer it, but see that it's a FaceTime when her face fills the screen.

"Why are you so close to the camera?" I ask her, laughing out loud.

She looks down and pulls it away from her face to a normal distance, giving me a sheepish grin. Despite that, her voice is cheerful when she answers me. "Well good morning to you too," she singsongs.

I rub a hand down my face. "It's like eight-thirty in the morning. How do you have this much energy already?"

She rolls her eyes and ignores my comment, clearly too excited to be bothered by it. "I've been up for hours trying to think of different ways to get you out of this situation those assholes put you in. But, of course, the internet wasn't really that helpful and I'm not a lawyer, so I don't understand half of that legal crap your mom was spewing at you. Then I tried to search *how to disappear without anyone finding you* and that took me to a weird and dark place on the internet that was not helpful at all, let me tell you—"

"Whoa, whoa, sounds like someone's had their fair share of coffee this morning," I chuckle, interrupting her because it's too early to follow one of her tangents. My smile fades at the same time I realize I should have been the one not getting any sleep by researching different ways to make this go away. Instead, I stuck my head in the sand, content to let my best friend deal with it. That thought settles in my stomach like acid.

"Okay, rude. I've only had, like, two cups this morning, but that's beside the point," she says.

"Uh-huh. Sure, it is."

"Well, I just thought you might be interested to know that I may have an idea, but if you want me to wait until later to share it …" she trails off, knowing full well she has me hooked.

I perk up at that. "And?"

"And," she continues hesitantly, biting her lip, "you may not like it, but it was the only thing I could come up with that could possibly work, so just hear me out, alright?"

"I'm listening," I reply tentatively.

"Okay, hypothetically speaking, if you could take Emma away from here, away from your parents and Adam, and leave your life behind, would you?"

I'm already nodding my head by the time she's finished speaking, not even bothering to think about the repercussions of what it means. "In a heartbeat."

She smiles at me and nods her head once. "That's what I thought."

I take in her smiling face and am slightly confused about where she's going with this. "But I thought you already googled *how to disappear* and got nada?" I say in a playful tone.

"Ah, not so fast," she says with certainty, holding her finger up in a dramatic pause. "You're forgetting that I'm a criminal mastermind. You still have your trust fund that your grandparents started for you, right?"

"Yes," I say slowly, "but I have to be eighteen in order to get it or else I would've done that already." I shake my head, still confused as to where this is going.

"True, but I also know that sometimes you can get it before you turn eighteen by having your parents sign over and transfer you your money," she states.

I contemplate that for a second, twisting my head from side to side. "Okay, I see where you're going with that, but there's still one big problem. My parents will never agree to transfer the money to me, especially after everything that happened yesterday. As soon as I ask, they'll know I'm trying to run and then I'll *definitely* lose Emma."

"Not necessarily." She smiles coyly at me while I narrow my eyes in suspicion. "Because you're not going to ask them. You're going to make a deal with them."

I shake my head at her notion. "And what exactly is this deal I'm going to make?"

"Well, you'll go to mommy dearest once we have the rest of the plan in place; it's imperative that you do this last," she tells me sternly, acting like this is some sort of covert operation. "You tell her that you've agreed to their terms, that you'll sign the papers for Emma's adoption, on the condition that you get your trust fund early for your cooperation. Tell her that you want to go on a shopping spree or travel somewhere, whatever you have to say, because you're sad about giving Emma up and this will help you feel better. Say whatever you have to, just make sure it's believable."

I bite my lip and look at the door. I know my parents can't hear this conversation—their room is on the other side of the house—but it still makes me nervous. This is a huge risk, one that can easily blow up in my face. I look back at Courtney and find her eagerly watching me, waiting for an answer. "And what if she doesn't believe me?" I ask her hesitantly.

"Well, you can always hit her with the cherry on top. Tell her that she can take possession of your car and phone until the court documents are processed and official, that way there's less of a chance you'll run without them. And as far as she knows, no one else knows about Emma, so she'll never suspect you have help." She shrugs casually over the phone, but I can see the determination in her face of how badly she wants this to work. How proud she is of herself for thinking of every possibility.

I think it over for a beat and can't believe I'm actually considering it. Although, I don't really have any other options at this point and I'm on very limited time. "That might actually work," I say slowly.

Courtney smiles at me triumphantly. "Hell yeah it might."

"What happens when I get the money, though?" I'm saying when, not if, because maybe if I put it into the universe, it won't blow up in my face exponentially. "Lest you forget, I won't have my phone or car, and I'm sure my mother will have me under lock and key until those papers are signed."

She's already nodding her head in agreement with me. "True, but I may also have a solution for that."

I raise my eyebrow at her. "Please, do tell."

"Do you remember my half-brother, Chase? He only came to visit that one summer a few years ago, but I swear you met him."

Of course I remember him, I immediately think to myself. He came to visit the summer Courtney and I had just turned thirteen. I remember how insanely hot I thought her older brother was at fourteen. With his shaggy brown locks the color of coffee falling into his piercing blue eyes, he couldn't have been any more stunning. Except that he seemed to have assholish tendencies, like pushing me in the swimming pool and making fun of my gap tooth during those long summer days. I also remember feeling incredibly guilty for crushing on him when I was already with Adam. I couldn't help wanting Chase to notice me, though, not look at me like his annoying little sister's friend, even though I knew it was wrong.

"Yeah, I think I remember him," I manage to say neutrally.

"I don't know if I told you this or not, I mean, you have been kinda busy keeping a human alive and all that, but he's actually living with us full time right now."

"Oh," I say, stunned, because I didn't know that. I try to rack my brain, remembering if she said anything about that, but nothing comes to mind. With that comes a pang in my chest, feeling guilty for neglecting our friendship. Sure, I've talked to her, but it was about everything going on in *my* life, not hers. I know she's right; I have been busy with Emma, but it doesn't excuse my actions.

"Hey, stop that," she says, her voice pulling me from my spiraling thoughts. She must be able to see the guilt I feel reflected on my face, giving me a sad smile. "I know what you're thinking, but don't. I know you have a lot going on at the moment, and I totally get that. It doesn't help that I'm not supposed to know about Emma and can't exactly just come over to spend time with you and catch you up on my life. But I hope you know I'm here for you no matter what," she tells me sincerely, and I feel my eyes misting over.

"I know that," I say. Bringing my hand up, I swipe at the lone tear that fell down my cheek.

"Good. Now that that's out of the way, back to my plan."

I smile at her, grateful for the reprieve, and sniffle away my remaining sadness. "Yes ma'am," I tell her with a fake salute that earns me a head shake in return.

"Anyway," she says, dragging the word out, "Chase has been staying with us since June, moving in right after his mom died. Dad didn't really tell me a lot of the details, but I know it was cancer. She had been sick for a while, so I don't think it was a shock to Chase or anything, but still."

Well, if that's not like a bucket of cold water being thrown over me, the teasing banter on my tongue swept right along with it. My chest feels hollow at the fact that I've missed what was going on in Courtney's life and for Chase, for the loss of his mom. "Poor Chase," I whisper before I can stop myself. Luckily, Courtney doesn't think anything of it, continuing to barrel on, determined to tell me her plan.

"I know, right? And evidently, he got strapped with like, a ton of her medical bills. Dad tried to help with her treatment and stuff, but Chase refused anything from him and now he has all this debt. I'm not sure what their agreement is, but suddenly he's back here, working for my dad, and completely miserable."

"Oh. Did he not want to go to college?"

"I guess not. He mentioned something about wanting to open his own garage one day, but I guess when his mom got sick his plans changed. That's one of the reasons he and Dad fight, and let me tell you, they fight *all* the time. That was why he hadn't come back to visit since that one summer, but we still kept in touch. He loves me but hates our dad, even if he won't tell me why. Anyways, I know he's been dying to get the hell out of this town, so I was thinking about a mutually beneficial relationship between you two."

"A what now?" I blurt.

"I know it sounds weird, but look at the facts. He hates it here and wants to leave, and you *have* to leave. He's been trying to save up money to open his own garage and you have lots and lots of money from your trust fund. He has a car to leave in and you don't. Getting it now?"

I inhale sharply. "Holy shit."

"Bingo." She smiles triumphantly.

"You're a genius," I breathe. I can't believe it. This might *actually* work. Neither my mother nor Adam have any idea Chase even exists. I never mentioned him to either of them when he came to visit that summer. Courtney is presenting me with a way out, a way to start fresh with Emma. I could give her an amazing life; one filled with love and acceptance. Something that I didn't have growing up. And Chase is my one-way ticket out of here.

"Do you think he'll agree to this?" There are too many different puzzle pieces that need to come together perfectly for us to pull this off, and Chase agreeing to it is key.

"I was going to talk to him about it today, but I wanted to run it by you first. I don't see why not, though." She shrugs. "He's miserable here and if he gets to leave by helping you, then I'm sure he'd do it."

"I really hope so."

"Okay, you said a week, right?" she asks.

I let out a sigh. "Probably less than that. The judge who's willing to authorize the papers is on vacation until Monday, so we have until then."

"Alright, then we'll have you both out of there by the weekend," she declares.

"Thank you. Seriously, you have no idea how much this means to me. I don't think I would have survived all this if it wasn't for you." I swipe at my cheek, not even realizing that I've started crying again.

"No." She waves her hand back and forth in front of her face. "Stop that. You are *not* going to make me cry. You know what an ugly crier I am."

I let out a teary laugh. "You're beautiful no matter what."

She rolls her eyes and shakes her head. "Liar."

"Love you," I say earnestly.

She smiles warmly at me in return. "Love you too. Forever and always."

"Forever and always," I echo softly.

I hang up and stare down at my phone until the screen goes dark, replaying everything we talked about. It sounds crazy, but I have a feeling that it might just be crazy enough to work. All I can do now is wait to see if Chase is on board with this wild plan. I look over at Emma and vow that no matter what happens, I need to trust that I'm doing the right thing for my baby girl.

CHAPTER 3

The days that followed my FaceTime call with Courtney passed by in a blur of furtive phone calls and secret planning. I learned that Chase was initially resistant to the plan, not that I could blame him. It was definitely an unconventional plan, and there was no reason for him to get involved with Emma and me; to help us out of a situation he had nothing to do with. But after a bit of persuasion on Courtney's part—because she can be very persuasive when she wants to be—he ultimately gave in. I didn't talk to Chase at all; Courtney was our go-between. Really, she was the one calling the shots, planning all the details out. Since I haven't seen Chase in years, I was both nervous and a little bit excited to see him. Courtney decided that we would meet on Saturday when my parents attended the annual back-to-school fundraiser, along with almost everyone else in town. It would be the perfect opportunity to make our "great escape" as she called it. I had rolled my eyes when she told me that but didn't contradict her. Thankfully, most of the kids at our school would be there, too, including Adam.

My mother easily accepted the lie that I fed her to get access to my money. I guess years of being a dutiful daughter helped in that regard. Plus, I knew exactly which strings to pull: my father. He had barely looked at me, let alone talked to me, since I broke the news of my pregnancy to them. I told her that I wanted to win back his trust and, *like the good daughter I was*, didn't want to go against their wishes. I told her that it would be a fair trade to get my trust fund early since I would be giving up my baby. I knew the moment she ran to tell my father the "good news"— that I was agreeing to their terms and would no longer bring "shame" to the family, as he put it—that I had them. The very next day my mother took me to the bank, where she signed every last cent of my trust fund over to me.

It's now finally Saturday, the day that we leave, and my nerves are going haywire. I chew on my thumbnail as I nervously pace around my room. I keep going over a mental checklist in my head, but I've done everything according to Courtney's plan. I just need to wait a few more hours until we can leave. I wring my hands together, my nervous energy bubbling up to the surface. I look around my childhood bedroom, knowing this will probably be the last time I'll ever be in here. I feel a twinge of sadness at that fact, but it comes and goes as fast as my next breath. They were the ones who put me in this position; forcing me to give up my baby. I won't feel guilty for what I'm about to do. Maybe when I'm older and this threat isn't hanging over my head, I can come back.

Just then, I hear footsteps nearing my door, followed by a few light taps on the wood. "Tatum, could I have a word?"

I rush over and quickly climb into bed. We have one shot for this plan to work, and it all depends on me staying home tonight. I figured the easiest way for my mother not to want me to go tonight is if I'm sick. I pull the covers up to my chin and toss a couple of crumpled up tissues on the bed around me.

"Yeah, come in." I holler at the closed door.

I pinch my nose a few times to get it as red as possible right as the door opens, revealing my mother, styled to perfection. Her hair is slicked back and tied in a low bun at the base of her neck. She's wearing an all-black suit ensemble that slightly reminds me of a businesslike Catwoman.

"What's up?" I try to say as casually as possible.

"Well, I wanted to talk to you about tonight," she says as she enters the room. I stay quiet while I wait for what she'll say next, knowing she will reprimand me if I interrupt her. "I was wondering if you would stay home with the baby." She cuts her eyes briefly to Emma before they settle back on me.

I quickly tamp down my excitement, not wanting her to see it on my face. Instead, I try to act bothered, as if this were the last thing I would want. "But why do I have to stay home?" I ask, whining for added effect.

She lets out a deep sigh as if I'm inconveniencing her and walks over to the bed. She sits down on the end of it, right by my feet, and fleetingly glances at the crumpled tissues surrounding me. Her nose scrunches slightly in distaste, her only sign of discomfort, before meeting my eyes. "Holly called and said she wouldn't be able to watch the baby tonight while we're at the back-to-school fundraiser. She has come down with a cold and is feeling very unwell. Seems that's going around," she says with disgust in her voice, her eyes flicking back over the tissues. That's the only acknowledgment I get about it. "It's probably for the best, though. With the Livingstons being mere days away from getting her, I wouldn't want anyone to accidentally talk. I know Holly is known for her … *discretion*, but I would hate for any confusion to arise."

It takes a tremendous amount of effort not to roll my eyes at her. Instead, I look down at my hands, hiding my smile. I wait a few seconds to reply, acting like I'm put out by what she's asking of me. I take a deep breath before looking back up at her. She has an eyebrow perfectly arched, waiting for my agreement.

"Fine, I'll stay here," I tell her solemnly. "I hate that I won't be able to go tonight." I look over at Emma, this time not bothering to hide the love reflecting in my eyes. "But I suppose it'll be good for me to spend these last few nights with her before she goes to her new home."

She beams down at me like it's the best news she's ever heard. Which, to her, I guess it is. Little does she know that Emma's new home will be with me, far away from here.

"There you go. Looking at the positives!" she exclaims. I offer her a shaky smile as she pats my leg before standing up. She starts to make her way out of my room but stops at the threshold and looks back at me.

"I'm happy you decided to listen to me, Tatum. Once this mess is behind you, you'll be able to go to all the events you want to. You can finally go to prom, since you missed yours last year. You have such a bright future ahead of you."

She stares at me, cocking her head ever so slightly, waiting for my reply. "Thank you. You always know what's best for me. I can't wait to enjoy my senior year."

She grins smugly at me, looking like she's never been prouder. I may have laid it on a little thick there, but I know that's what she wanted to hear. Without bothering to look at Emma, she walks out, pulling the door closed behind her and leaving me in silence once again. I slowly blow out the breath I was holding and sink into the mass of pillows behind me, knowing that now I just need to get through the next few hours without any problems.

My mother never comes back to my room after that, but I do see her a little while later in the kitchen when I'm making a bottle for Emma. She comes strutting in, with her blonde curls pinned away from her face, cascading down her back. She's wearing a floor-length, bright, emerald-green dress with a high neck in the front and lower in the back, stopping just under her shoulder blades. Her high heels clack against the marble floor as she walks by me, and I do have to admit that she looks good. Not that I would ever tell her that, nor does she need to hear it; she knows just how good she looks and has the confidence to back it up.

"Ah, Tatum, there you are," she says when she spots me in the corner. "Your father is already waiting in the car, and we can't be late. We gave Maria the night off, so you'll have to make something yourself I'm afraid."

"That's okay, I can manage. Have fun tonight." I tell her with a tight smile.

"We will."

She dismisses me with a nod as she turns on her heel and leaves the kitchen, her dress swishing around her ankles as she goes. I wait, frozen on the spot, until the sound of her high heels fades away, and I hear the distinct echo of the front door opening and closing. I take my time making Emma's bottle before glancing at the clock. Ten minutes after seven. That means I only have about thirty-five minutes to feed Emma and finish packing our things before Courtney and Chase arrive. Not having my phone to check in with Courtney makes everything a little more difficult. Although my mother believed me, she still took my phone away like we suspected she might. "You will get it back once you sign the adoption papers." She told me. I knew that was a strong possibility, so I didn't mind; Courtney and I had already planned everything out that we needed to. It's a slight risk, leaving soon after my parents did, but I didn't want to wait any longer. The quicker we left, the more distance we could put between us and here.

I race upstairs with Emma's bottle and quickly feed her. A glimpse at the clock on my desk as I'm burping her lets me know I'm now down to five minutes. I groan and carefully place Emma in the middle of my bed. "I'll be like two seconds, sweet girl. Please don't go rolling around," I beg.

Once I'm sure she's not going anywhere, I go to the back of my closet, moving some of my hanging clothes aside to get the suitcase I hid back there. I bring it to the foot of my bed and open it up, then go to my bathroom to grab the small toiletry bag I stored under the sink. I place it on top of the clothes I've already packed in the suitcase and zip it up. I quickly run over to Emma's room and grab her diaper bag off the floor. I place the baby monitor in it, along with her white noise machine, diapers, and a little stuffed giraffe I bought right after I found out I was pregnant. I made sure to only pack the essentials in my big suitcase—we can stop to get anything else we may need once we're on the road. Finally, as fast as I can, I collapse her portable crib and pack it into its holder.

Emma gives me a gummy little smile and babbles from her spot on the bed when I walk back into my room, like she's proud of herself for not moving. "You're such a sweet girl, aren't you? Listening to your momma," I coo at her. "I'm just going to get you strapped in, okay, and then we're going to go on a little adventure."

I buckle her into her car seat—the one I brought her home in —and throw the diaper bag on my back. I wrap my hand around the car seat handle and walk down the stairs with her. Once I reach the foyer, I set the car seat on the floor and slide the diaper bag off my shoulders, placing it next to Emma. I race back upstairs to grab my big suitcase and Emma's portable crib and awkwardly make my way downstairs with them. Even though I tried to pack as light as I could, it's still a lot for me to carry.

Just as I'm placing the bags next to Emma's car seat, I hear a light tapping coming from the back door. I startle and pause for a second, my heart racing thinking maybe Adam has somehow caught me. I slowly walk over and peek around the corner to see Courtney waving frantically at me through the glass doors. I shake my head and go to unlock the door.

"What are you doing at the back door, you weirdo?"

She rolls her eyes at me and steps through. "I was just taking precautions. I wanted to make sure no one saw me come over here." She gives me a once-over and smiles. "It's good to see you."

I can't help it. I yank her in for a hug, and she wraps her arms around me, hugging me back just as fiercely. "God, I missed you." She pulls back and holds me at arm's length. "Motherhood looks good on you," she says with a wink.

I roll my eyes and knock her hands away but smile all the same. My smile fades, though, when I look around her and see that it's just her here. "Where's Chase?" I question, trying not to panic.

"Oh, I told him I'd text him once the coast is clear and then he'd pull the car up. He's waiting around the block for now." I let out a sigh of relief as she pulls her phone out of her pocket and starts typing away on it.

"My parents left just a little bit ago. Hopefully everyone else has as well and no one calls the cops on some stranger sitting in their car on our street." I laugh half-heartedly, attempting to make light of the situation. Then I bite my lip. "I haven't looked to see if Adam and his parents have left yet, but they're never late to anything so they should already be there."

Courtney looks up at me and shakes her head. "I didn't see anyone when I was walking back here," she replies and hesitates for a second, as if debating to tell me something. "I, uh, did see a picture of Adam on Instagram, though. At the fundraiser. He was in one of Staci's stories." She taps a few times on her phone and then hands it to me.

I take it from her, and that slow rage that had been building earlier comes racing back to the surface. In the picture that was posted, Adam has his arm thrown over the shoulder of one of his friends, there's a bunch of them together, while his other arm is wrapped around Staci. They're all smiling or laughing, obviously having a good time, while glasses of champagne hang from their fingers. He's out there, enjoying his life, completely unfazed at the fact that our daughter is about to be taken from me. I close my eyes briefly before handing Courtney her phone back. She pockets it with a sympathetic smile on her face. I shake off my ill feelings I have toward Adam and smile up at her.

"Come on. I want you to meet Emma."

She follows me to the foyer where Emma is in her car seat.

Courtney exhales roughly when she sees her. "God, she's perfect, Tatum."

"Do you want to hold her?" I ask.

She looks at me with glassy eyes and nods her head frantically. I had wished for this moment for so long. For the moment when my best friend would finally be able to meet my daughter in person. Courtney could only ever see her over FaceTime or from the pictures I would send her. I unbuckle Emma from her car seat and gently hand her to Courtney.

"Holy shit," she whispers in awe, staring down at her. Then she looks up at me with wide eyes. "I mean shoot. Crap. I'm sorry."

I laugh at her. "It's okay. Technically she doesn't understand curse words yet."

I let them have their little moment, with Courtney holding Emma in her arms, telling her how she can't wait to spoil her rotten and take her shopping once she's old enough. It's unspoken, but I know what she really means is once the threat of my parents and Adam isn't looming over us anymore. Suddenly, there's a loud knock at the front door, interrupting this special moment.

Assuming that's Chase, I go over and open the door. I look up and up to find that standing before me isn't the scrawny boy with shaggy brown hair I remember. Instead, there stands a guy with a muscular build, his toned arms on full display in his short-sleeved T-shirt, who's taking up way too much space in my doorway. His hair is cut shorter around the sides but still messy on top, almost like he's run his fingers through it a couple of times. It's somewhat darker than I remember, and his eyes are a brighter blue than before. I'm momentarily stunned by this new person in front of me, feeling like all the oxygen has been sucked out of the room, that I forget to form any sort of greeting. Before I'm even able to, a slow smirk forms on his mouth.

"Well, if it isn't Tatum Rothchild, all grown up."

"Chase, be nice," Courtney chides, walking over to us with Emma still in her arms.

"So," he nods towards Emma, "this is her?"

"Yup, this is Emma," I reach out to her and her little hand wraps around my index finger with her gentle grip. "My daughter."

I glance back at Chase, trying to gauge his reaction.

"She's cute." He stares at her for a few seconds before looking at me, and I try to imagine what he sees. The last time we saw each other, I was thirteen with my gap tooth and barely developed boobs. Like him, I've grown up too. My chest filled out and a retainer helped fix the gap, making it barely noticeable now. And, of course, I now have a baby. I'm a far cry from his annoying little sister's friend that he seemed to never want to be around.

"We should probably get on the road instead of standing around." His rough voice interrupts me from my musings.

"Yeah. The sooner you all leave, the more distance you'll cover before they notice you're gone," Courtney agrees, and I nod my head eagerly.

"Yeah, no, totally. I just fed her, too."

"Alright then," Chase says, grabbing the suitcase and diaper bag and heading out the front door.

I reach out and take Emma from Courtney's arms, bending down to fasten her back in her car seat. Once she's secure I straighten up right into Courtney's outstretched palm. I glance down and notice a little black device in her hand. I tilt my head and shoot her a questioning look.

"What's this?"

"A burner phone."

I take it from her hand and turn it over, examining it. "Huh. I've always heard about these, but I don't think I've actually seen one before. It looks just like a normal phone."

Courtney snorts. "That's because it basically is, except it doesn't have any apps. All you can do is call or text. I already programmed my number on it, just in case, and prepaid for unlimited minutes for 60 days. It's completely untraceable, too, so your parents won't be able to track it." She bites her lip and looks up at me tentatively. "Please text me once you're settled and let me know that you're safe."

I reach out and pull her into a tight hug. "I will, I promise. Thank you for this. For everything you've done for me." I whisper into her hair. Her coconut-scented shampoo engulfs me, and I blink a few times to keep the tears at bay, knowing how much I'm going to miss her.

Before she can reply, Chase comes back inside, interrupting our moment. "The car's all packed. Just waiting on you and Emma," he tells us.

I let go of Courtney and step back. "Right. Of course."

I grab Emma's car seat and follow Chase and Courtney out the door, locking it behind me. Once I get the car seat secured in the car, I give Courtney one final hug goodbye. Even though I know we should be getting on the road, I let myself have this moment with her. When we break apart, I rub a hand across my face, wiping the tears away, hating that I have to say goodbye to her. One look at her and I can tell she feels the same—silent tears streaking down her face.

"I'll see you soon, okay?" she says with a shaky voice.

With a sniffle and a nod, I wipe my nose and offer her a wobbly smile. "Yeah, I'll see you soon."

She shakes her head at me. "Besides, you can't keep me away from my goddaughter for long."

I can't help but laugh at that. "Duh, she'll miss you too much,"

I say, conscious of the fact that we're talking about more than just Emma.

She nods in Chase's direction. "And take care of him too, will ya."

"You ready?" Chase interrupts before I have a chance to reply. I look over my shoulder and find him leaning against the car, his forearms braced in front of him on the roof.

"I will," I whisper to Courtney.

Chase and I get into the car, and I reach into my purse to grab my wallet.

"Oh, before I forget, here you go." I hold up five prepaid Visa gift cards. "I was able to get my trust fund transferred onto my own separate account at the bank, but I didn't want to risk using my card and my parents finding us. So, I transferred a large amount onto several of these prepaid cards. These are yours—to help pay for everything on the trip—then once you drop us off, I can give you the rest."

He grabs the cards from my outstretched hands and puts each one in his wallet. "Thanks. Courtney didn't, uh, tell me how much money you had, just that I'd get a cut?" He poses it like a question, shifting in his seat to look at me.

I give him a tight smile. "Don't worry, it'll be enough to open your own garage."

He raises his eyebrows in surprise. "Okay ..." he says slowly. "And we'll be good with these cards for the trip?"

"Should be. I transferred a thousand dollars onto each of them."

He nods and starts the car. He doesn't say anything else while he shifts the car into drive. A bittersweet feeling washes over me as we drive around my parents' U-shaped driveway. It's the fact that I'm leaving the only home I've ever known. Leaving my parents, my friends, my school—pretty much everything— behind for this little girl sleeping in the backseat. Except with all that sadness comes the realization that I know I'm doing the right thing here, and I would do it again in a heartbeat.

"Thank you. I haven't been able to tell you how much this means to me."

He shrugs. "No problem. Besides, it's easy money, right?"

"Right." I force a tight smile while a lump forms in my throat at the realization that I'm paying someone who is basically a stranger to go on this road trip with me. Still, I know this is the right thing to do.

Chase slows the car as we turn onto the street and I roll my window down. Sticking my head out, I take a final look back at the house that I might never see again. Courtney raises her arms above her head and waves at me. I wave back, not stopping until we've gone down the street and her outline slowly fades away. It's only when I can't see her anymore—when I've rolled my window up and turned back to stare at the endless night before me—that I finally let the tears I've been holding fall.

CHAPTER 4

Our drive started out terribly uncomfortable. For the first hour, neither of us spoke, too lost in our own heads. Or, at least, I seemed to be. Thankfully, I had stopped crying shortly after we left. I could tell Chase wasn't sure what to do or say to me because he kept glancing over at me with furrowed brows every so often. Whether it was out of annoyance or concern, I didn't know. Ultimately, I was glad he didn't try to offer me any comforting words or advice—I probably wouldn't have accepted it anyway.

After a little while, it occurred to me that I had somehow unintentionally let him take over. I never thought to ask where we were going; I just expected him to get us there. But I guess, in a way, isn't that the whole point of this endeavor? I'm providing the money, and he's providing the getaway car. I mean, isn't that what Courtney had said?

Finally, after much internal debate, I turned to him, breaking the uncomfortable silence, and asked where we were headed. He had briefly glanced at me before returning his eyes to the road. At first, I thought he wouldn't reply from the long pause that followed, but he surprised me by saying, "Figured we can start by going south for a bit and then head west. I don't really have a destination in mind, though." I just nodded like that was a solid plan, even though I felt way out of my depth.

He told me he bought a map right after agreeing to our plan, knowing that neither of us would have a phone with working GPS and would have to rely solely on a map. I had taken it out of the glove box and kept it in my lap, feeling more secure in my role as the passenger. I know it didn't make much sense, but for some reason, I didn't want him to think I couldn't handle this— that I wasn't smart. Although, I was pretty sure he already thought that every time Emma cried and we had to pull over so I could feed her, even if he never said anything. He also rarely asked for directions. The only time he would ask for my help was when he needed to know where a gas station was because we hadn't seen a sign for miles.

And that's how we end up here, pulling up outside a motel in the middle of nowhere, Pennsylvania, just a little after one in the morning. Chase tells me to wait in the car while he goes to the front office. After a few minutes I see him striding back towards the car, so I get out and immediately stretch out my limbs, my body stiff from sitting for that long.

He holds up our motel key. "We're in 103." He indicates with his head to a door only a few doors down from us.

"Okay," I say and get Emma out of the car.

With Emma in my arms I fall in step behind him, and we walk towards our room for the night. We stop at a flimsy door with the number 103 on it, although the three looks like it's barely hanging on. He slides the key in, twisting the lock, and flips the light switch on. He briefly scans the room and, seeming satisfied that there's no danger lurking in the shadows, ushers us inside. As I step over the threshold I glance around, noting that there's not much to it other than the two small beds and a round table in the corner. I expect to see a TV or a dresser, but there's nothing. The wallpaper decorating the walls looks like it's been here since the eighties, with it peeling in some places and completely faded in others. The dirty brown carpet has definitely aged as well, looking like it hasn't seen a vacuum in a while. Averting my eyes from that disaster, I look around and relax when I see there's a shower, sink, and toilet. At least they have the essentials. Except I quickly glance back at it, confused for a second. It takes me a moment to realize the problem. The toilet is right next to the sink, but it's just sitting there, in the room, without anything around it. There's no door or curtain to hide it. I blink, not quite believing what I'm seeing. This place seemed to take the whole "open space" concept to another level. I almost snort at my joke, but I'm still too baffled by the situation to do so.

"There's no bathroom." I blurt.

Chase, who just locked the door, glances up at my statement. His eyes narrow as he surveys the room again, taking it in with a keen eye this time. His nose wrinkles when he see the would-be bathroom and absentmindedly runs a hand over his chin, no doubt trying to come up with a solution.

"They told me this was the only room available," he mumbles to himself. He walks over to the window and pushes the curtain aside with one hand, eyes scanning the parking lot. "Although I don't really see how considering there are only two other cars here."

I wave him off, not wanting to make this a bigger deal than it needs to be. "It's okay. We can, um, just tell each other to look away when we have to go?" It comes out more of a question than I intended it to be. I'm suddenly nervous about standing here in this room with him. Not because I don't trust him, but because this feels a lot more intimate than I expected.

He gives me a strange look, almost as if he didn't believe that would be my answer. I mean, I get it, I do. Just a year ago, the idea of me being a teen mom on the run with a guy I barely knew, would have been absolutely laughable. Because there was no way that I, Tatum Rothchild, would ever stay in a place that wasn't a five-star resort. Yet, here I am, stuck in a dingy motel room, discussing our bathroom situation with said guy. Oh, how drastically life can change.

"You sure?" he asks, still giving me that funny look.

Since there's nothing else we can do at this point, I shrug. "Yeah, it's fine. It's not like we have a ton of options."

He nods and looks around again, eyes scanning over the room. "Yeah, I suppose you're right." He rubs the back of his neck uncomfortably before swinging his gaze back to mine. "So, we'll just let each other know then, okay. I'll go get our stuff from the car."

Before I can offer to help him, or say anything else for that matter, he's out the door. I let out a breath as soon as the door is shut, thankful for the small reprieve his absence is providing. It's as though I haven't been able to breathe until right this second, feeling the weight of the last few hours heavy on my shoulders. I instantly regret taking a greedy gulp of air after because as soon as I do, the smell of moldy ashtrays fills my nostrils. I wrinkle my nose and try not to gag as the door swings open and Chase saunters back in, arms loaded with our things.

"Thanks," I tell him when he hands me Emma's portable crib. I get her crib set up and try not to flinch every time I touch a dust-covered surface.

Chase clears his throat suddenly. "I'm going to, uh—" I look over and see him make a spinning motion with his index finger, indicating he wants me to turn around.

"Right," I say, feeling a blush creeping up my neck. I try to ignore the sound of his steady stream and the rustling of fabric as he changes his clothes. It's a strange feeling to be in the same room with Chase as he undresses. I've seen him in swim trunks, and even though I'm not looking at him right now, just knowing he's right there has somehow put me on edge. I mentally chastise myself and shake my head to clear my thoughts.

Once he's done, I grab a diaper from Emma's bag and change

her. Then I put on her nighttime onesie and lay her down in her crib. Knowing it's my turn, I dress and take care of business as quickly as possible, trying to avoid looking in Chase's direction. I can't help stealing a glance at one point, though, and find him sitting on his bed with his back to me. At least we have separate beds because despite how I'm trying to handle the whole *making it work* thing, I don't think I'd be able to handle anything else right now. Small mercies, I suppose.

Exhaustion has taken over by the time I crawl into bed and slip under the covers. I take extra precautions not to pull the sheets up by my face and try to ignore the way they itch my skin. It helps that my mind is still reeling from today's events. I can't stop the images of leaving my parents' house from replaying on an endless loop. I toss and turn, not fully comprehending that this is real. That somehow, I'll go back to that house and laugh about how I almost pulled one over on them. But this is real. I know what I did really happened and there's no coming back from that. I know that I'll wake up tomorrow in this dingy motel with its 60's-style floral-patterned bedspread and its unsavory, stained carpet. I release an involuntary shudder at what this motel has seen before us and instead focus on Emma's sleeping form in her crib. And despite the place we're currently in, despite flipping my life completely upside down, I fall asleep with a smile on my face, knowing that she will have the best life I can give her.

The following two days pass by in a blur of motels, gas stations, and fast food. I feel like I could explode from all the greasiness we're consuming. Still, we don't have the luxury of wasting time by stopping to eat something that takes longer than ten minutes. We already do that enough to feed Emma and change her diapers. Traveling with an almost five-month-old is no joke. Sometimes, I have to sit in the backseat and entertain her with a few her toys. It isn't ideal, but we don't have any other options. I'm proud of her for the most part, though; she only truly gets fussy when she needs a diaper change or is hungry.

I still haven't been able to get a good read on Chase. The only times we really talk are to discuss when we should stop or where we should stay. Usually, we just sit listening to whatever is on the radio. There's no idle chitchat or getting to know each other. I'm not looking for us to become best friends or anything, but whether he likes it or not, we're in this together.

I can feel myself getting more agitated by the minute thinking about it, so I'm thankful when Chase slows the car down and pulls into a gas station parking lot.

"I'm just going to grab an energy drink. You want anything?" He asks.

"I'll come in with you," I blurt before I can think better of it. Chase quickly does a double take. I know he's surprised by my answer since every time we've stopped previously, I've chosen to wait in the car. It's not like I didn't want to get out and stretch my legs, but one, I was terrified my parents had someone trailing us and I'd be spotted, and two, it can be a hassle to unload Emma each time we stop, and one of us needs to stay in the car with her. I'd rather Chase be the one to get out since he's taking the brunt of the work by driving all the time. Plus, it makes more sense for me to avoid places with cameras, just in case. It sucks, but I am kind of on the run after all.

Chase continues to stare at me with his hand on the door handle. Without giving away a hint of what he's thinking. he slowly says, "I thought we agreed it was best if you wait here?"

I sigh. "Yeah, I know we did, but I'm tired of being cooped up. I want to get out, just for a minute," I plead, sticking out my bottom lip just a hair. I know I don't need his permission, but I'd rather not rock the boat. "Plus, aren't we far enough away by now that we should be fine?" I tack on, uncertainly.

Chase sighs, dropping his hand from the door handle and

leaning back against his seat. He glances over his shoulder at Emma. After a moment, he turns back around and leans forward slightly, his head tilting as he studies all the angles of the gas station. I'm assuming he's looking for cameras, and I try not to squirm in my seat as I wait to see what he'll do next. I almost squeal with giddiness when he finally shakes his head and relents, shutting off the engine.

"Fine, but we're in there ten minutes max," he says sternly. My cheek twitches, trying to hold back my grin at his serious expression. So, I do the next best thing and salute him.

"Yes sir," I tease.

He rolls his eyes and shakes his head, mumbling something under his breath that sounds suspiciously like the word *brat*. He opens his door and gets out of the car while I scramble to undo my seatbelt and do the same. I go to the back door and unbuckle Emma, lifting her into my arms and wrapping my cardigan around her. That's another thing I've learned about Chase; he likes to keep the car cold. I have to bundle up like it's winter instead of the middle of August.

Chase walks in front of us and opens the door, motioning us inside. I mutter my thanks and he follows us in. I'm thankful I decided to keep my cardigan on because a blast of cold air hits me as soon as I step inside. I eye the restroom sign in the back corner and bite my lip. I pause instead of making a beeline for it like I really want to do. This isn't something I've tackled with Emma yet, and I'm worried it will be too much of a hassle. I'm contemplating how long I can hold it when I hear Chase's deep rumble from behind me.

"Give her to me."

I turn around and shoot him a quizzical look. "Huh?"

"I can hold her while you go to the bathroom," he says, nodding to the sign behind me, obviously seeing the indecision warring on my face.

I hesitate. "Are you sure?" I ask. It's not as though he's ignored Emma really, but this is the first time he's offered to hold her.

He nods again. "It'll be easier for you to go without her."

"Oh, um, okay. Thanks." I hand her over to his outstretched and waiting arms.

I glance back as I walk into the alcove under the restroom sign, just long enough to ensure they're okay, before slipping into the bathroom. I quickly take care of business, not wanting to burden Chase longer than necessary. I head back out but my steps falter, and I come to a halt right under that dang restroom sign. Because when I look up, I immediately spot the two of them by the drink cooler, Chase holding Emma so carefully in his arms. My breath catches in my throat, and my heart does a little flip at the sight of them—how normal it looks to see him holding her like that. Instead of rushing back like I planned, I take my time walking towards them, wanting to savor this moment. As I pass by the candy aisle, I make a rash decision and grab a pack of Twizzlers. After I have them in my hand, I look around and find Chase leisurely strolling up the different aisles. I take a deep breath to steady the onslaught of nerves and walk up behind them.

"Thanks for watching her," I say once I reach them.

He hastily turns around, a slight smile curling the edge of his lips. He looks relaxed and carefree for a moment before schooling his features. "Not a problem."

We stand there for a second, both of us staring at each other before I finally come to my senses and shake it off. "Here, I've got her," I say as I reach out my free hand and take her from his arms. Without warning, Chase grabs the bag of candy from my other hand and any protest I might have dies on my lips at his smug smile. His eyes roam over the Twizzlers and he raises an eyebrow.

"Twizzlers?" he asks with a smile in his voice.

I narrow my eyes at him. "Hey now, don't talk bad about Twizzlers. They're a classic."

He huffs a soft laugh under his breath. "No, it's not that. Just some things never change."

I tilt my head and furrow my brows in confusion. He starts to turn away, giving me his back, but I'm not letting him go that easily. "What's that supposed to mean?" I ask before he can walk away.

He glances back at me over his shoulder and shakes his head as he turns around to face me. "It's nothing. I just remember you always had a pack of Twizzlers with you when you were hanging out at my dad's house." He shrugs and stares off to the side of my face, not making eye contact with me.

"You remember that?" I ask softly.

He scoffs and meets my eyes. "How could I not? You were obsessed with them."

"Oh, whatever." I roll my eyes and push past him, needing to put some distance between us. He's not wrong; I used to eat Twizzlers all the time when I was over at Courtney's house. So much, in fact, that she had stashes of them all over the kitchen and her bedroom that were just for me. But it's the fact that Chase somehow paid enough attention to remember that; something I barely even remember because I haven't eaten them much since that summer. I shake my head slightly, hoping to clear these thoughts that I don't know what to do with and make my way to the front counter.

Chase follows closely behind me, his footsteps echoing on the linoleum floor. I readjust Emma in my arms when we reach the front counter and stand slightly off to the side as Chase puts my candy, two bottles of water, and an energy drink on the counter. An older man steps up behind the register when he spots us and begins ringing up our things. He gives us a once over, his gaze lingering on Emma for a second too long as he continues to scan the items. He looks up and catches me watching him, giving me a wink with a crooked smile that sends a thin shiver down my spine.

"Cute baby," he croaks, sounding like he smokes a pack a day.

I furrow my brows and shift uncomfortably while holding Emma tighter to me. I wish I could cover her completely with my cardigan so he won't look at her anymore. "Um, thanks," I reply uneasily.

"Y'all kids travelin' alone?" he rasps, staring at us intently with wide eyes, his yellow teeth poking out when he talks.

"Yup," Chase nods, thankfully replying to him since I don't want to. The guy gives off major creep vibes. "Going to visit some family," Chase adds.

"Oh? Where y'all headed?"

Chase glances at me briefly before looking back at him. "Florida."

The man shakes his head. "Ah, e'rybody wants to go to Florida." He starts putting the candy and drinks into a bag on the counter as he talks. "Not me though, no, too hot for me down there. Ya gotta make sure you have plenty of air conditionin'. Y'all got air conditionin' in ya car?" He squints as he looks up at Chase.

"Sure do," Chase says as he pulls out his wallet from his back pocket and swipes the Visa card.

"Well, that's good." The man smiles big, showing off his yellowing teeth once again, and I try not to visibly cringe at the sight. Chase just nods politely and picks up our bag off the counter. We make our way to the door, but stop just shy of the exit when we hear his raspy voice call out from behind the counter.

"Y'all be careful on your way to Florida, now. A lotta bad things can happen to kids like y'all. Make sure not to go stoppin' for no one, 'kay?"

I turn back to him against my better judgment, and find him leaning far over the counter, his forearms braced against the surface as he watches us. A shiver rolls through me again right as I feel an arm wrap around my waist. I look up to find Chase pressed against me, his frame surrounding Emma and me, his eyes focused solely on the man. He holds the man's stare a beat longer before tugging me to follow him out the door, his arm still firmly around my waist.

He doesn't let go until we reach the car. He opens the back door for me while I buckle Emma into her car seat. Chase is rigid next to me, watching the front of the store like he's guarding us, and for that, I'm thankful. It isn't until I'm safely buckled in my seat with the door shut that he walks around the car and gets in, turning the key and starting the engine. We peel out of the parking lot as fast as we can and Chase keeps glancing out the rearview mirror, even as we get farther and farther down the road. Finally, I break the silence.

"That was weird, right?"

Chase glances over at me but says nothing, his grip on the steering wheel tightening.

"Do you think he recognized me?" I ask suddenly, panicking at that thought. It hadn't crossed my mind until now, but with how he stared at me, what if he did? Of course, the one time I wanted to just get out of the car could be the time that I'm caught.

Chase shakes his head, replying, "No, I don't think so." His eyes dart to the rearview mirror again. "I think he was just a creepy old redneck."

My heart rate slows back down to normal with his words. I'd rather he not somehow recognize me enough to report back to my parents about where we're headed. Which reminds me.

I glance at Chase. "Why did you tell him we were going to Florida?"

He sighs. "Because if anyone miraculously finds out we were there, then your parents will think you continued to go south and go on a wild goose chase. While fortunately, we'll already be heading west."

I blink at him, bewildered. "Oh. That makes sense."

He hums in agreement but doesn't say anything else. I'm still surprised over the fact that he offered to hold my daughter and the way he seemed protective of us back there. I hate to admit it, but even though I had a slight crush on him that one summer, after that —when he never came back to visit—he seldom crossed my mind. I got swept up in my own life, just like I'm sure he did his. But now I'm curious about what he's been up to for the last four years.

"So, Courtney never said, but I'm assuming you already graduated?" I ask casually.

His eyes flick to mine briefly before returning to the road. It takes him a few minutes to reply, and I can see his jaw working as if he really doesn't want to answer me. Like he hopes that if he waits long enough, I'll forget I even asked a question. Well, *too bad*, I think. I continue to stare at him until he finally relents. He exhales and replies, "Yeah, last year."

I smile triumphantly. "That's cool. What was the name of your high school?"

He cuts his gaze to me again. "Why do you want to know?"

"Just curious, I guess." I shrug and bite my lip, starting to feel self-conscious.

He narrows his eyes at me curiously, but answers sooner this time. "Red Crest High School. Down in Texas."

"Oh, you stayed in Texas?" I ask excitedly.

He does a double take. "You remember I lived there?"

I roll my eyes, fighting a smile. "Of course. I thought that was the coolest thing. All the cowboys and rodeos, it must have been so much fun."

He lets out a small laugh and shakes his head. "I lived in North Texas. We didn't have much of that there."

"Oh," I feel myself slightly deflate at that and mumble, "still seems cool though." I relax back in my seat and stare out the window, watching the trees go by, waiting for him to ask me a similar question. I figure he must have a burning curiosity about how I ended up in this situation, but the question never comes. After what seems like forever of counting mile signs—twenty-two to be exact—I get bored. I roll my head to look over at him and squint my eyes. "So ..." I drawl, "did you play any sports?"

He glances at me, his eyes connecting with mine, and raises an eyebrow. "What is this, twenty questions?"

I huff, determined not to feel defeated by his constant dismissal of me. "Well, what else are we supposed to do?" I throw my arms up in the air. "We still have who knows how long of a drive ahead of us and we've barely talked. What's wrong with wanting to get to know each other?"

He shrugs again. "Don't see a reason to. We knew this was going to be a long trip, but I have one job. I just want to get you and Emma to your new home safely. That's it. Then I can get my payout, and we can go our separate ways."

An air of finality envelopes us, clinging to me while a new wave of sadness overwhelms me. I turn my head and look out the window so he won't see me struggling to hold back my tears. His words shouldn't hurt—this was the plan we agreed on before we left, after all—but it still stings all the same. I thought that maybe this trip wouldn't be so hard, that maybe we'd form a friendship, and I wouldn't feel so alone. But it's clear that he doesn't see it that way. To him this is just a job. Suddenly I'm back to being his annoying sister's friend, no more than a slight inconvenience for him, and I don't know how to feel about that.

CHAPTER 5

It's later that evening, the sun slowly setting beyond the horizon, when we pull up outside an actual hotel. From the outside, it looks like one of the nicest places we've been to on our trip thus far. Although that's not saying much, considering that all the places we've stayed at have been small, grimy motels. Though none were as bad as the first night, they weren't a huge upgrade either. I can't help but feel a little excited. Maybe this place will have soap and sheets that don't scratch you at night. It's not the smartest move, no doubt this place has security cameras, but it's the only option we could find for miles.

Chase pulls into the parking lot and parks in the back corner, away from the entrance and any streetlights. "Wait in the car while I check us in."

"Okay," I say, knowing the drill by now.

He leaves the engine running and gets out of the car, his head bowed with a baseball cap pulled low over his forehead. He makes his way to the entrance of the hotel, which is only four stories tall, with beige stucco all around the sides and a tan roof. The windows are small, and the portico by the front entrance looks like it could crumble at any moment, but overall, it seems to be in good shape. After a few minutes Chase's tall figure exits through the doors and saunters up to the car. He gets in the driver's seat and twists around, rummaging through the backseat for something. He turns back around and holds up a dark blue baseball cap.

"Wear this," he says as he tosses the cap to me. I don't have time to catch it, so it flies through the air and lands in my lap with a small thud. "And make sure to keep your head down and avoid looking at the cameras."

"Got it." I grab the cap from my lap and secure it on my head, trying to tuck as many of my blonde locks underneath it as I can. The soft fabric is stretched from wear over time and sits loosely on my head. I reach back to tighten it, but it has one of those brass clasps that you have to pull it through, and I struggle to get a hold on it.

"Here, let me." His hand brushes against mine and I quickly pull back, feeling like my skin is on fire from where he touched it. He leans closer to adjust the hat, and I get a whiff of his cologne. I breathe in deeply, inhaling the scent of woods and spice. I wonder if it's him or the hat, but either way, I enjoy the feeling of it wrapped around me. "That good?" he asks, bringing me back to reality.

"Yeah, thanks," I say quickly, a blush spreading over my cheeks.

He doesn't say anything as he leans back in his seat, readjusting his own hat so that it sits a little farther down on his face. He turns the engine off and gets out of the car, slamming the door shut behind him. Keeping my head down I follow his lead, getting Emma unbuckled from the car seat while he grabs our bags from the trunk. I trail behind him as he leads us away from the front entrance and toward the back door. He swipes the hotel card and the little black box flashes green, letting us in. We only walk past two doors before he stops in front of what I'm assuming is our room. I try to keep my head down, staring at the floral pattern of the carpet, until I hear a click and am ushered inside the room. It's not much, but at least it smells clean. The bed is neatly made and looks like it has fresh sheets, too. And that's when I do a double take. I turn my questioning gaze to Chase, who is busy putting our luggage down.

"Uh, I thought you got a room with two beds?"

He looks back at me in surprise, and I watch as he takes in the room. As soon as his eyes land on the *one* queen bed, he exhales sharply and curses. "I did. Shit. I think they gave us the wrong room," he groans, sliding his hand down his face. "I'll go get this sorted. Be right back." He starts to leave, but I stop him before he reaches the door.

"Did you tell them we were staying here, too, or just you?"

He glances back at me and I can tell from the look on his face that he didn't breathe a word of us to the person at the front desk. "Just me," he confirms.

I tilt my head. "Wouldn't that kind of be a problem if you complain about only having one bed? You can't exactly demand two beds if it's just you. That could be suspicious, right?"

He crosses his arms over his chest and leans against the wall. "Okay, what do you suggest, then?"

I look around the room again, noting that the only other furniture is a desk and a chair, and I'm not making one of us sleep in a chair. "Look, it's fine. One of us can just sleep under the covers, and the other one can use a blanket if they have one. We can even make a pillow wall if it makes you comfortable." I shrug and look at him, the shock of my suggestion evident on his face with the way his eyebrows shoot up in surprise. I smile up at him. "It'll be fine. Come on, we're both adults here."

He gives me a look.

"Ish," I add. Because we both know that if I were a legal adult we wouldn't be in this situation to begin with. "I mean, we did survive the toilet saga. This is nothing," I say, trying to lighten the mood.

He uncrosses his arms and pushes off the wall, stalking towards me. "You okay with that?"

"Yeah, totally. It's no big deal." I lie nonchalantly. Maybe if I keep telling myself that, then it will be.

He nods. "Okay then."

He goes over to where our bags are and starts setting up Emma's crib. I sit down on the bed, Emma still in my arms, and watch him work. Emma's tired eyes following his movements. Her sleep schedule is messed up at this point, but I'm doing the best I can with our given situation. Chase finishes with the crib, placing it at the foot of the bed. He rubs the back of his neck nervously, his eyes meeting mine for a moment before glancing away.

He clears his throat. "The lady at the front desk mentioned there's a good diner a few blocks away. I figured if you're tired of fast food, maybe we could check it out?"

I blink a few times at what he just asked, hating the way my heart skips a beat at the idea of going to dinner with him. He's only asking me because we need to eat and really, he's right. We can't live off fast food forever.

"Yeah, that sounds really good actually."

His shoulders relax at my answer, and I narrow my eyes slightly at him. A few hours ago, he said that we shouldn't get to know each other, yet here he is asking me if I want to go to dinner. I shake my head, not even wanting to try and understand what is happening in that head of his.

I don't know what to expect when we pull up outside the diner, but it isn't this. Large bay windows showcase the hustle and bustle happening inside the diner, while string lights adorn the gravel parking lot and a large neon diner sign hangs above the front entrance. Our shoes crunch along the gravel as we make our way inside, and a bell over the door dings when Chase opens it. An older woman in a light blue waitress uniform calls out from behind the counter, telling us to sit wherever we'd like. I'm only half listening to her because I've stopped to take in the startling scene before me.

It feels like we've stepped right back into the fifties. Red and white booths line the side walls and there's a long white countertop in the middle that spans almost the entire length of the diner with circular, turquoise high-top chairs positioned underneath it. Behind the counter is a large cut-out opening that reveals the kitchen and the two cooks working hard over a set of flat-top grills. I watch in fascination as waitresses refill coffee cups and bring out plates piled high with fries and delicious-smelling cheeseburgers.

"Come on," Chase's voice pulls me back from staring at the workers and I realize he's already walking toward a booth in the far back. I pull my cap down over my face as much as I can and head that way.

My shoes squeak on the black-and-white checkered floor as I follow him, and I can't help but continue to look around, captivated by the allure of this diner. There's even a small jukebox tucked into a corner by the end of the long countertop, playing upbeat jazz music. Vibrant lights illuminate the top edges of it, pumping out different colors in time to the beat of the music. I slip into the booth across from Chase and place Emma's car seat beside me, tucking her between me and the wall.

"Well, what do you think?"

I cut my eyes to Chase and find him already watching me intently. I smile as I look around the diner, taking in the lights and colors. Even Emma seems mesmerized by the atmosphere, if her little babbles and wide eyes are anything to go by. "This place is amazing."

"Right? I'm glad the lady at the hotel told us to come here," Chase replies.

I look at him and am momentarily blinded by his smile. He watches me closely, and his smile seems happy and genuine—one I haven't seen before. For a moment I find myself at a loss for words. It takes my brain a few seconds to remember what he said, and as I start to reply, a young woman wearing the light blue waitress uniform, probably in her early twenties with bleached blonde hair and hazel eyes, walks up to our table.

"Hi there folks! My name's Macy and I'll be taking care of you this evening. Can I get y'all started with anything to drink?"

She looks at me first. "Just water, please."

"You got it. And you?" She looks at Chase expectantly.

"Same for me."

"Alrighty, I'll bring that right out for y'all," she replies with a smile.

She hurries off, leaving us to sit in silence in her wake. Chase sits with his arms folded over his chest as he takes in the diner, watching everyone come and go. I unclip Emma from her car seat and hold her in my arms. I bounce her lightly as her wide eyes stare up at the ceiling, the light from the jukebox entrancing her. She babbles and waves her hands in the air, loving the different colors. Chase watches us silently and leans back in his seat. He drops his keys on the tabletop, the clinking sound momentarily startling Emma. For a second he looks scared, probably thinking she'll have a complete meltdown, but I know better.

"Uh-oh," I tell him. "You've done it now." Emma stretches her arms out in front of her, immediately wanting his keys. He looks at me for guidance, confused about what to do. "You can shake them for her. She loves anything that rattles."

He hesitantly picks up the keys and rattles them in front of her face. It's not long before he starts laughing as she tries to grab at them. She finally gets a hold of them and gives a little baby laugh, sending Chase a big, gummy smile in return.

Chase gives me a half smile. "I think she likes me."

I look away from where Emma's sticking the metal keys into her mouth and up at Chase. "And how do you know that?"

"She's smiling at me," he says as he nods at her.

I roll my eyes. "Babies smile at everything."

He scoffs, but before he can say anything, Macy comes back with our waters and sets them on the table. Her face breaks into a wide smile when she spots Emma in my lap.

"Oh my gosh, that is like the cutest baby ever!" she exclaims, gushing over her.

I smile and look down at Emma, who's as comfy as can be, creating small spit bubbles in her mouth and watching the waitress with sleepy eyes. "Thank you."

"Y'all are such a cute family."

Chase chooses that exact moment to take a sip of his water. He quickly sputters, coughing slightly as some of the water dribbles down his chin. He wipes off his mouth with his hand as he answers her. "Oh, no, that's my sister." My head snaps to him in shock, but he suddenly refuses to meet my gaze.

"Oh, I'm sorry. I just assumed," she says awkwardly, and I don't blame her. "Do you, uh, know what y'all would like to order?"

"I'll just have the cheeseburger with fries." I mumble.

Chase lets out another quick cough, clearing his throat. "I'll take the patty melt with fries and a side of bacon, thanks."

Macy smiles at us, but it's forced. "I'll get that in and have it out to y'all shortly."

She quickly leaves and we're left alone again in uncomfortable silence. My cheeks heat as an intense feeling of embarrassment and rejection burn in my chest.

"Sorry, I didn't mean—" Chase starts to say but I wave my hand to cut off whatever excuse he's come up with.

"Don't worry about it."

"Tatum—" he tries again, but I refuse to let him continue.

"Chase, seriously, it's fine. Saves us from having to explain it,"

I say, hating the words on my tongue. But he doesn't owe me anything and he doesn't need to play family with me—especially with a pretty waitress like Macy smiling at him.

He gives me an apologetic look, like he wants to say more, but I refuse to meet his gaze. Instead, I stare down at Emma and watch as her sleepy eyes flutter closed. I gently lay her in her car seat so she can sleep while we're eating. Macy brings our food out soon after with as little interaction as possible. I'm a little surprised by that. I thought now that she believed I was his sister she would have free reign to flirt with him. Still, even with her keeping it professional and Chase not paying any more attention to her, I've lost my appetite. I push the fries around my plate, having only taken a few bites of the burger, no matter how delicious it smells.

"Is the food okay?"

I look up, expecting Macy to be there, but it's not her who asked the question; it's Chase. I guess he noticed that I wasn't really eating any of it. I look and see that almost all of his patty melt and fries are gone.

"Yeah, it's good. I guess I'm just not really hungry after all." Before he can say anything else I stand up suddenly. "I need to go change Emma's diaper."

I slide out of the booth and grab Emma's car seat and her diaper bag. Her sleepy eyes pop open at the sudden movement and I quickly locate the sign pointing to the restrooms, not bothering to look around the diner at anyone else. I push open the door to the ladies' room and look around for a changing table. Thankfully, I find one in the far stall, and I get to work changing her diaper.

"Yeah, you had a stinky diaper, didn't you?" I say to her when I take off her dirty diaper. That's what I get for feeding her and not changing her diaper before we left the hotel. She grabs her feet in her hands, making noises as I finish up. I toss the dirty diaper in the trash and wash my hands at the sink inside the stall. After I'm done, I brace my hands on the counter and stare down into the sink. I try to take a few deep, calming breaths, but it's no use. My chest feels like it's tightening, restricting the air into my lungs, and tears prick the back of my eyes. For the first time, I wonder if all this was a mistake. I'm angry that I was put in this position by Adam and my parents, and I'm frustrated at myself over the fact that I'm upset Chase called me his sister. It shouldn't matter, and yet, it does.

I shake my head. This is my path now, and the only thing I can do is move forward. Turning on the faucet, I cup my hands under the cold water and splash some on my face. Grabbing a few paper towels, I blot my face dry. My eyes look a little red, but it's the best I can do. Sighing, I throw Emma's bag over my shoulder and buckle her into her car seat. As we're walking out of the bathroom, I don't make it more than three steps before I bump into somebody. Luckily, I'm able to steady myself before we both go crashing to the ground.

"I'm so sorry."

"Oh my gosh, I'm sorry." We both say at the same time.

I look up to see the person I collided with was Macy, our waitress. She smiles at me sheepishly. "That was totally my fault, I wasn't paying attention to where I was going. Is she okay?" she asks, nodding towards Emma.

"No, it's okay. I wasn't exactly looking either. And yeah, she's fine," I say, feeling a little self-conscious and slightly embarrassed the longer she stares at me. "Well, I should probably get back …" I trail off, hooking my thumb over my shoulder in the direction of the booths. I turn and start walking away when I hear her call out to me.

"Wait!" I turn as she comes to a stop before me. "I just wanted to say I'm sorry again for how I reacted to y'all earlier. I felt like a big ole' dummy for calling y'all a couple like that. I tend to put my foot right in my mouth." She makes a wild gesture with her hand aiming down at her foot and then up to her mouth. I smother my laugh at that. "Anyways, I guess I just got kinda embarrassed and wanted you to know."

I smile warmly at her. "It's okay, it wasn't that big of a deal."

"That may be, but I just feel creepy for sayin' that ya know?" She shivers. "We tend to get a lot of jokes about that down here and I don't want y'all thinking we play into that stereotype or anything."

She looks at me with such seriousness that this time I do laugh. "Trust me, we don't think that."

"Ya sure? It's just 'cus—"

"We're not actually related," I blurt, deciding to put her out of her misery.

"You, huh?" She cocks her head at me and squints her eyes. "But he said—"

"Yeah, I know what he said. He's actually my best friend's older brother, so I guess he sees me like a little sister but, uh no, definitely not related." I shift uncomfortably as I tell her that.

"Oh," she says, and relaxes in obvious relief. She smiles at me. "Well now that makes more sense."

Now I'm the one that's confused. "What makes sense?"

She waves me off. "Nothing. Sorry, sometimes I just say whatever pops into my mind, just ignore me."

I'm already shaking my head. "Why does it make sense that we're not related?" I press.

She shrugs. "It was just the way he was watching you when you weren't looking. It seemed more like how someone would look at the person they love, not their sibling." She shrugs again, this time looking a little uncomfortable at admitting that.

I take an automatic step back as if she slapped me, my mouth hanging open slightly, because none of what she just said makes sense. She notices my discomfort and her face gets bright red.

"Oh my gosh, seriously just ignore me. I stuck my foot in my mouth again, didn't I? Why do I do this to myself?" she mumbles the last part mostly to herself.

She hangs her head and props her hands on her hips. I reach out and touch her arm lightly before she spirals. "No, you didn't. I just think you were seeing something that's not there is all. He doesn't see me like that."

She stares at me for a beat and then shakes her head. "Yeah, you're probably right. I should get back to the kitchen." She turns to go, but then stops and looks back at me. "What was your name?"

"Tatum," I reply automatically without thinking.

"Well, Tatum, just so you know, y'all would make a really cute couple." She smiles at me and then disappears through the door to the kitchen.

I stand there for a moment, staring at the empty spot where she was, more confused than ever. She doesn't know what she saw, making up this romantic scenario in her mind. I shake my head, trying to clear the thoughts of us being a couple from my mind. Chase said it himself; once this is over, we go our separate ways.

I make my way back to the booth where Chase is sitting with his arms folded on top of the table, his fingers drumming an invisible beat.

"Everything okay?" he asks as I slide into the booth.

I startle. "Huh?"

He looks at me with concerned eyes and a furrowed brow. "I asked if everything was okay. I saw you talking to the waitress." He nods over to where I was standing and his eyes roam over me.

I nod. "Yup, all good. She was just talking to me about Emma," I lie, because I definitely don't want to tell him how she said we'd make a cute couple. "You ready to go?"

He looks down at all the food still on my plate. "You don't want to finish that?"

I shake my head no. As much as I want to, I don't think I could stomach it after that weird conversation I had. I'm torn between getting butterflies of excitement and a nauseous feeling of dread. Chase narrows his eyes at me but relents.

"Okay. I've already paid the bill, so we're good to go whenever."

"Thanks."

We both slide out of the booth simultaneously, and I lean over to grab Emma's car seat. As we walk out, I take one last look around this incredible diner. It's a shame I didn't enjoy it as much as I wanted to. I hate that my emotions got the better of me and ruined what could have been a fun and exciting night. Everyone else seems to be enjoying themselves—from the older couple sipping their milkshakes to the group of friends tossing fries at each other. In another life that could have been me hanging out with my friends on a Friday night, cuddled up next to Adam, joking around without a care in the world. Without having to take care of a baby.

For a fleeting moment, I yearn for that version of life. But just as quickly as I have that thought, it fades away. That isn't my reality anymore and I've accepted it. As mad as I am at my parents and Adam, I'm also thankful. Because even though it's scary, I'm excited about this adventure we're embarking on— finally being able to decide what I want for my life without anyone else trying to dictate it for me. To become the mom to Emma that I wish my own mother was to me. Promising to put her first and always making sure she knows how loved she is. The only hurdle left is figuring out how I'll survive who knows how long on the road with Mr. Grumpy Pants over here. I can only hope the rest of our time together will go much smoother than it has been.

CHAPTER 6

The next morning, I wake up after one of the most restless sleeps of my life. I don't understand how Chase managed to sleep so comfortably throughout the night, but he did. And I know this because I could hear his steady breathing and soft snores as I lay next to him, curled up under the covers. We stuck to our agreement. Chase grabbed a blanket from the closet as soon as we got back from the diner and told me he'd use it so I could have the bed. I tried not to toss and turn all night, but that proved difficult. Instead, I found myself lying still, staring up at the ceiling, my eyes refusing to close.

Sometime in the middle of the night, though, I did manage to fall asleep. It was one of those sudden sleeps, where I closed my eyes and didn't even realize I had dozed off. Then, I awoke suddenly to Chase turning over or moving around, fully aware that I wasn't alone in the bed. Even Emma was able to sleep through the night. So, that leaves everyone but me feeling refreshed, and I wake up looking like a zombie. I'm sure Chase notices the dark circles under my eyes and my pale skin but is kind enough not to say anything. I feel like I'm floating underwater as we make our way to the car, my hair piled low under my cap and my cardigan pulled tightly around me.

"It looks like we need to go about 300 miles further and then we're all set to go west the rest of the way," Chase's muffled voice breaks through my fog. I pry my eyes open to squint at him, the morning sunlight blinding me through the windshield. He's holding the map, concentrating hard on the route.

"That works," I mumble sleepily.

He cracks a smile and looks over at me. "You tired?" A hint of laughter fills his voice.

I don't bother responding. My eyes slowly start to droop, and I don't have the strength to fight it anymore. I close my eyes and relax back against the seat before slowly drifting off to sleep.

A slamming door jolts me awake and I look around, slightly panicking and trying to get my bearings. I see that we're stopped at a gas station and Chase is outside, leaning against the car as he pumps gas into it. I turn around to check on Emma and find her babbling away, playing with one of her toys. It's a fabric book, and she's waving it up and down, her tiny, chunky arms cutting through the air. She has her pacifier in her mouth that wasn't there when we left earlier, and I can only assume Chase gave it to her. I turn to find him placing the nozzle back into the holder, then opens his door and gets in.

He smiles when he sees me. "You're awake."

"Yeah, sorry about that. How long was I asleep for?" I rub my hands over my eyes, wiping away the remnants of sleep from them. He starts the car and as I'm sliding my hands down my face the dashboard lights up and I'm finally able to see what time it is. My eyes bug out at the same time Chase replies.

"About four hours."

"Oh my gosh how did I sleep that long?" I turn to look at Chase, my eyes still wide with shock. "Why didn't you wake me?"

He shrugs. "You needed the sleep." He looks over at me and smirks. "You kind of looked like the walking dead this morning."

I swiftly reach over and smack his arm without even thinking. "I thought you weren't going to say anything about that!"

He just laughs. "Nah, how could I not? Plus, watching you drool was the best part." He uses his index finger and gestures at the corner of his mouth, indicating drool coming down.

"Wait what? I don't drool!" I exclaim and hastily wipe my hand over my mouth, attempting to get any of the drool off in case he's right. I look at my palm but there's nothing on it.

He lets out a full laugh from watching me scramble to wipe my mouth and even though it's at the expense of me, I shake my head and laugh along with him. Once our laughter dies down, he holds up his hands in surrender.

"Sorry, I'm just messing with you. You don't drool." A slow smile creeps across his face, "but you did snore a little."

He laughs again at his joke and this time I simply roll my eyes at him. "Okay, okay, I get it. I'm a horribly tragic person when I'm sleeping." He looks at me warmly and smiles, making my traitorous heart skip a beat. I clear my throat and look away. "You done?"

"Yup," he says. "Oh, I almost forgot." He grins smugly and reaches around to the back seat and grabs a plastic bag with a gas station logo on it. "Figured you might be a little hungry when you woke up."

He hands me the bag and I peek inside to see an assortment of some of my favorite snacks. I spot the Twizzlers almost immediately and reach in to grab the family-sized pack he got me. Ripping open the plastic I snatch a red rope out of it, biting down to release a burst of strawberry flavor.

"This is the best thing ever. Thank you," I say with a big smile after I'm finished chewing. It's not even about the snack itself that has me smiling so wide, it's the fact that he remembered and got this for me. He doesn't say anything, just nods in acknowledgement, as he starts to shift uncomfortably in his seat.

"Oh crap. I need to feed Emma!" I say suddenly. The long nap

I took has completely thrown off my timing off because she should have already been fed by now. In fact, I'm a little surprised I didn't wake up from her crying because she was hungry.

"Actually, I already fed her."

Chase's words stump me, and I actively deflate back in my seat, not expecting that. "You did? When?"

"Right before you woke up." He juts his chin to something just beyond the car. "I made her a bottle and fed her over there on the picnic bench." I turn to follow his line of sight and see a single wooden picnic table set up on a grassy area beside the gas station. A red umbrella is positioned through a hole in the middle of the table, covering the space in shade. There's a few cigarette butts on the ground around it, but other than that, the place looks relatively clean. I narrow my eyes and look back at Chase.

"How did I sleep through that and not know?" I say more to myself.

He shrugs, answering me anyway. "Like I said, you needed the sleep."

I'm stunned as I stare back at the picnic bench, trying to picture what it must have looked like to see him feeding her. He must have been paying attention to how I've fed her all the other times before because I've never showed him.

"Thank you, I really appreciate you doing that for me."

He waves me off. "Don't worry about it. I, uh, didn't change her diaper though. I'm not exactly sure how to do that," he says.

"Oh, that's okay, I've got it. I probably should go to the bathroom while we're here anyway."

I get out of the car and lift Emma from her car seat, cradling her in my arms. With my head tilted down, we walk inside the small gas station. After changing her diaper, I quickly take care of my business, not wanting to take too long. After I'm done, we head back outside and I'm careful to avoid looking at any security cameras they might have. I get Emma settled back into her car seat before getting into the car myself.

"You ready to hit the road again, sleepyhead?" He asks with a tilt of his lips when I buckle my seatbelt.

I smile and sit back to get comfortable in my seat. "Ready." He puts the car in drive and gets back on the road, a cloud of dust kicking up behind us from the dirt parking lot.

It's a little while later, when the sun is finally beginning its descent into the horizon, casting an orange glow over everything, that we stop at a motel we spotted along the highway. Chase veers the car into the parking lot. I open the door and swing my legs out, inadvertently knocking a bag full of fast-food wrappers from the floorboard out onto the ground. I cringe at the sight of it, knowing I won't be able to last much longer on burgers and fries. It's only a matter of time before my skin starts breaking out, not being used to this much grease. All I can do is sigh as I reach down and pick it up, tossing it back onto the car floor before shutting the door closed. I don't have the energy to deal with that right now— that'll be a problem for another day.

Chase has our bags unloaded by the time I get Emma out of the car, so I adjust my hat with my free hand and follow him to where the front desk is. I keep my head down and wait for him outside the office, subtly peeking through the glass door and windows as he talks with an older woman. She looks bored out of her mind, staring at Chase with a glazed-over expression as he hands her the card. After running it she hands him the key and his card. He slips the card into his wallet and puts it in his back pocket as he walks towards us. I watch as the woman goes back to reading whatever gossip magazine holds her interest. A musty smell drifts out as Chase opens the door and I wrinkle my nose, hoping this won't be as bad as some of the other places we've stayed at.

I stare at the ground as we walk along the concrete path in

front of the many motel doors and up the stairs. I'm still trying to keep my face away from cameras, worried that my parents might have hired a private investigator to find me. I start to wonder what excuse they have come up with as the reason for my disappearance. I know how important it is for them to keep up appearances, so I can't help but be curious about what they've told people.

Sometimes I forget that we're still very much on the run, instead getting swept up into our own little road trip bubble we've created. Even though we still don't talk too much during the drive, it's beginning to feel more comfortable than it did before. To be fair, I'm used to it for the most part. I was never one to be a social butterfly at all the parties I had to attend with my parents. Usually, I just stood there, hoping I could fade into the background. Adam was the one most people talked to; he understood the social politics at those types of events.

The key turning in the lock on the door pulls me from my thoughts and I shake off the last of that self-pitying feeling and survey the room. It's like most of the other ones we've stayed at so far. Although the hotel we were at last night was much nicer, I'm thrilled to be back in a motel—solely for the separate beds. I don't think I can handle another sleepless night of lying next to Chase. It makes me aware of the boundaries that are slowly blurring and the need for the wall that Chase puts up. Because as he's said before, when this is over, we'll go our separate ways … and I need to remember that.

I set Emma's diaper bag on the round table in the corner knowing that I'll need to change her diaper right away. I'm not a complete snob, but I still find myself quickly grabbing one of the towels from the bathroom and adding it under the changing blanket I have, just in case. You never know what could be on there. I start changing her diaper and freshen her up with some wipes. After I'm done, I throw the dirty diaper away in the trash can under the sink and put her into her onesie. I pick her up in my arms and turn around to find Chase in one of his basketball shorts and white T-shirt sleeping combos he wears every night. His shirt tonight has some red and gold logo I can't quite make out. I must've been so preoccupied with Emma that I didn't even hear him change.

"Could you grab her mat out of her bag for me and put it on the floor? I want to get some tummy time in since she's been in the car so long."

"Sure." He rummages in her bag and takes out the purple and white mat, laying it on the carpet at the foot of the bed. I gently lower her down on her tummy, and she giggles, slapping the mat with her hands. Chase sits cross-legged on the floor beside her, a smile tugging at his lips. I grab one of her rattling toys and hold it in front of her, her little arms reaching out to grab it as she babbles at us.

"Uh-huh. You like the rattle, don't you?" She gives me her gummy grin, continuing to babble. "Yeah, but you like your giraffe even more." She giggles and I laugh with her, loving how happy she seems.

Chase reaches out and softly touches her arm. He looks up at me. "I can watch her and put her to bed if you need to take a shower or anything."

I glance at him. "Are you sure?"

"I don't mind," he says as he smiles down at her. "We're good, aren't we?" Emma babbles in response. "See? Told ya."

I laugh. "Okay, well, I'll try not to be too long. She only needs about five more minutes of this and then she'll be tired enough you can put her in her crib."

He nods. "I got it."

"Thank you," I tell him. I grab the nightclothes I've been wearing from my suitcase, and wander into the bathroom. When I get into the shower, I stand under to the hot water for a few extra minutes before scrubbing my body down with the bar of soap. My fingers briefly brush against the stretch marks lining my stomach that I love so much. It's always a powerful reminder that this body created and carried my whole world. After all, it's what brought me Emma. I smile as I rinse the suds off and hop out.

As I'm sliding my soft night shirt on, a musky smell hits my nose that I'm pretty sure doesn't belong to the motel. I reach down and pull the top of my shirt up to my nose and sniff. My face scrunches up when I realize the musty smell is indeed coming from me. I groan with the realization that I wore this same shirt last night and pray that I didn't smell this bad then. Or that if I did, Chase didn't notice. We're really going to have to stop by a laundromat and wash our clothes soon, or at least buy some new ones so we can keep moving, because the smell of us will only get worse.

When I walk out of the bathroom, I spot Chase propped up against the headboard, staring down at Emma. He's on the bed closest to the door and window, leaving me to sleep in the bed next to the bathroom. It's become somewhat of an unspoken rule that we do this, him taking the side closest to the door. I've always wanted him to be the first to choose since he's the one driving all the time. Plus, Emma sleeps next to my bed and I assumed he would want her farther away from him in case she woke up. This time is different, though. Instead of putting Emma on the other side of my bed, he put her in the crib he set up between our two beds.

"Emma's here?" I ask a little nervously, though I'm not sure why.

His eyes don't stray from the crib as he answers me. "I figured it'd be easier for her to be here." Finally, he looks up at me, but his face is blank, giving me no indication of what he's thinking. I swallow hard and just nod my head in agreement.

"Makes sense." I barely manage to rasp.

I feel his eyes lazily following me as I saunter over and flip the light switch down, plunging us into darkness. I wait a second for my eyes to adjust and clumsily feel around until I get to my bed and crawl in. My body feels exhausted as I'm pulling the covers over me, and despite already sleeping for half the drive, I feel myself start to drift off. Just as my dream state threatens to pull me under, a loud horn blares from outside our room. Chase shoots up and is out of bed in seconds flat, throwing the covers off unceremoniously. He rushes to the window beside his bed and pulls back the curtains.

"What is it?" I ask. I sit up halfway, propped up by my pillow.

He shakes his head. "I'm not sure. I can't see anything."

I bite my lip as he stares out the window, trying not to worry. What if my parents have found us somehow? Of course, if they did, I doubt they'd honk. They'd probably send a SWAT team in to break down the door. Chase continues to survey the parking lot, but after about a minute of silence, he lets the curtain go and walks back to his bed. The curtain falls against the window, once again covering us in darkness. I try to relax, telling myself to stop being so ridiculous. We're safe here with Chase. He's just starting to gather up his covers when the horn sounds again. He stumbles in his haste to get to the window and pulls the curtain aside to look out once again. At the same time, Emma lets out an ear-piercing wail, startling us both. We both turn and look at her before I jump into action, reaching over her crib and scooping her up in my arms. I bounce her lightly, as much as I can while still sitting on the bed, since my nerves are a wreck. Meanwhile, Chase has already returned to the window.

Chase sighs in relief after a moment. "Looks like it's just some drunk guy in the parking lot picking up a friend."

I scoff. "And he felt the need to blare his horn?"

He shrugs and looks back at me. "No clue."

I roll my eyes in annoyance and bounce Emma in my arms until her crying subsides. I whisper in her ear, "It's okay, it's okay. I got you, girl," until I feel her tiny body start to sag against me as she drifts off back to sleep. Chase lets the curtain go and sits on the end of the bed, hunched over slightly with his forearms braced on his knees. I reach over with my free hand and turn on the lamp next to me, needing a little light to help settle my nerves as I continue to lightly bounce Emma. When I look up, I find his blue eyes already staring back at me. I clear my throat and quickly look away.

"Should we try and find another motel to stay at in case this happens again?" I ask him, breaking the silence.

He's already shaking his head by the time I finish speaking. "No, I don't know where another one is that's nearby and I don't want us to be traveling this late at night. Plus, the room's already paid for."

I scrunch my brows in confusion. "There's plenty of money."

He nods and sighs at the same time, swiping a hand down his face. "Yeah, I know there is, but we need be smart, Tatum. We don't know how much longer we'll be on the road for and we don't need to be spending money unless it's necessary," he says, frustration clear in his voice.

I sit up straighter as irritation and embarrassment flow through me. "I realize that, *Chase*, I'm not a child—"

"Never said you were," he interrupts snidely, shaking his head.

I roll my eyes at his comment, feeling my defenses going up. "I just meant that I don't want Emma to wake up crying every freaking hour if that continues," I whisper-yell, pointing towards the window with my free hand to indicate the noises. Chase opens his mouth as if he's going to say something before quickly snapping it shut. He runs his fingers through his hair, and I can't tell if he's gearing up for a fight or just fed up with me. Instead of arguing, though, he sighs.

"I can go down to the front desk and see if they have a radio or something that could drown out some noise in case it happens again?"

I stare at him, completely stunned for a second, not expecting him to say that. "Um, yeah, I—" I start to tell him to go ahead and do that, but then remember that I snagged Emma's white noise machine from my parents' house when we left. I never mentioned it before, not wanting to overwhelm Chase, but now seems like the perfect opportunity to bring it up. I bite my lip in hesitation before finally answering. "I, uh, I actually have Emma's white noise machine that used to be in her room. That thing practically drowns out every single noise. It's in her bag."

He raises his eyebrows, surprised by my answer. "Oh. Do you want to use it, then?"

I nod wordlessly and get out of bed, my mind reeling from everything that happened in the last ten minutes. I gently lower Emma down into her crib and walk over to the table and dig through her bag. Almost immediately I spot what I'm looking for at the bottom of it and retrieve it, zipping the bag closed. I take the noise machine out of its box and plug it into the outlet underneath the table. As soon as I turn it on, the soothing sound of waves crashing against the shore fills the room, accompanied by a soft white glow that offers a hint of a nightlight as well.

When I turn around I find Chase already tucked into bed, waiting on me. Hoping this works and we can all sleep through the night, I climb back into bed. I reach over and flick off the lamp beside me, except we're not encased in total darkness this time. Just as I start to let the waves lull me to sleep, I hear Chase's quiet voice pierce through the noise.

"She slept with this on every night?" he grunts.

"Mmhmm," I reply sleepily.

"Why haven't you been using it then?"

I crack my eyes open at his surprisingly jarring tone. "I guess I just thought it would disturb you at night," I mumble lamely.

"Yeah, but if it helps her sleep then I wouldn't have minded," he says, his voice cutting through the dark. I don't have to see him to know he's probably looking at me with those attentive eyes.

I whisper back softly, "That's okay. Besides, she's using it now." I shake my head and mentally want to slap a palm on my face. What kind of answer was that? He doesn't answer so after a while, I assume he fell asleep.

I roll over on my side, facing away from him. Right as I start to get comfortable under the covers, I hear him whisper, "Goodnight, Tatum."

A smile creeps across my face. "Night, Chase," I whisper back. I snuggle deeper into the bed, smile still plastered on my face, and finally drift off to sleep.

The noise machine seems to work its magic because the next morning we all wake up much later than usual. I let out a big yawn as the sun streams in through the window, and a quick look at the old clock on the bedside table alerts me to the fact that we're typically on the road by now. Not that I mind; it's nice getting to sleep in a little bit without having to rush out the door. Even Chase seems to be in a good mood, stretching his arms high above his head as he saunters to the bathroom. I hear him brushing his teeth and figure now's a good time to get up and get Emma ready for the day.

I'm finishing changing her diaper when he comes out of the bathroom, already dressed and freshened up, his wet hair hanging in his face from his brief shower. "I'm going to see if anyone at the front desk can tell me if there's a good coffee place somewhere around here. I'm starting to get tired of those watered-down gas station ones."

I nod my head and smile at him. "Okay. That sounds great."

He leaves and I put Emma back down in her crib while I quickly get dressed and brush my teeth. I decide to skip a shower, knowing Chase will be back any minute and we need to get going. I'm packing the rest of my things in my suitcase when I hear a *ding* come from somewhere inside the room. I freeze, my heart beginning to race as I try not to panic. I know I'm alone in the room, but I realize I also forgot to lock the door after Chase left. I look back at my suitcase, and it suddenly hits me. It's the phone Courtney gave me. I dig around my suitcase until I find it in one of the zipped pockets. I take it out and blink down at it. Courtney's the only person who would have this number, and I'm curious as to why she would be texting me now. Especially since I told her I wouldn't text her until I'm settled.

I hastily read over her message and my stomach clenches, a sense of dread filling me. Out of all the things we had planned for, this wasn't something I anticipated. I debate whether to respond or what to even say. I absentmindedly chew on my thumbnail as I pace around the room, weighing my options, when I hear steps growing closer outside the room. I look up at the sound of it, figuring that Chase is back, and quickly pocket the phone in the back of my jean shorts. Chase walks in just as my arm drops to my side.

He gives me a puzzled look, probably wondering why I'm standing in the middle of the room staring at him. "Looks like there's a coffee place about a mile down the road." He tells me, hooking his thumb over his shoulder before dropping it and tucking his hands into the pockets of his jeans.

"Cool," I say, hoping I sound somewhat normal and he doesn't hear the way my voice slightly shakes.

He tilts his head and studies me for a beat as I force what I hope passes for a natural smile. "You didn't lock the door." He nods his head behind him indicating the door.

My eyes flicker over to it and then back to him as he watches me. "Oh, I totally forgot." I cringe, already knowing I should've locked it. "I was busy changing Emma and then trying to pack ..." I trail off, waving my arms in front of me.

"You're all packed up then?" He glances around the room to see Emma still in her crib and my open suitcase.

I walk over to the suitcase and zip it closed. "Yup. Just gotta get her crib and load it into the car."

I bend down and grab the handle of the suitcase to drag it up, but rough hands brush against mine as Chase stops me. "I got this. Why don't you and Emma head to the car." He poses it more like a statement than a question so I nod in agreement.

"Yeah, sure, I can do that."

I worry my lip between my teeth as I grab Emma and head out to the car, Chase following behind us. I try to act normal while wondering how to tell Chase about the text I got from Courtney. The drive to the coffee shop is a short one, with a grand total of one traffic light in this small town. We pull into the gravel lot and park directly in front of the coffee shop. My eyes roam over the small, hut-like building with its red, tin roof slanting downwards over a tiny, square window cut out in the center of the painted glass, which I'm guessing is where we order from.

I turn and look at Chase. "Do you mind if I wait here while you get the coffees?"

"Sure. What would you like?"

I debate for a second before answering. "Uh, pumpkin spice latte if they have it," I say with a smile.

He looks at me with a furrowed brow. "You do realize it's August and still hot outside, right?" A hint of a smirk plays across his lips and his eyes hold a glint of humor in them.

I school my features and give him a blank stare. "And your point is …?"

It takes all of two seconds for me to burst out laughing, unable to keep my serious expression. He shakes his head at me but is smiling all the same. "Alright, one pumpkin spice latte it is."

A wide grin stretches across my face as he exits the car. I lean over the seat and yell an exaggerated "thank you" just before he closes the car door. I'm still smiling as I watch him shake his head again and, even without seeing him, I know he's rolling his eyes too. Laughing to myself, I sit back in my seat and see a young guy about my age slide the window open and start taking Chase's order. It only takes a few minutes before Chase is walking back with two large coffees. He places one of the cups on the car's roof before he opens the door and hands me the other one. I take it from him and hold onto it as he grabs his cup, slides in and puts his own coffee in the cup holder.

"One pumpkin spice, just for you," he tells me once he's settled into the seat.

I hold in my squeal of happiness at finally getting a pumpkin spice latte and instead blow into the opening on the top of the steaming paper cup. "Thank you."

"You don't have to thank me. It wasn't that big a deal," he says flippantly, already putting the car in reverse and pulling out of the parking lot.

"Right," I whisper, though I don't know if he heard me or not.

We're both treading carefully as we navigate this oddly intimate situation we've found ourselves in. Still, that doesn't mean I don't appreciate everything he has done for me. I know if I tell him that, though, it might not go over very well. I've learned that Chase is the kind of person who does what he does because he wants to, not because he feels like he has to. That's what I keep holding onto—the fact that he continues to do these thoughtful things for me, and for Emma, because he wants to. That's the big difference between Adam and him. Adam always wanted to be acknowledged for the things that he did, making it an automatic response that I now have.

I take a big gulp of my coffee, letting the warmth of the pumpkin fill me as I moan in delight. The nerves I once had about the text from Courtney slowly disappearing. That is, until I hear another *ding* and remember the burner phone I still have in my back pocket. I swallow hard, refusing to look over at Chase to gauge his reaction. I shift in my seat and with trembling hands pull the phone out of my pocket and glance at the screen. I realize that I'm caught now, and I need to tell Chase why she's texted me.

CHAPTER 7

I feel Chase's eyes boring into the side of my head, but I keep my gaze locked outside the window, watching as the trees get sparse. I know he's curious and wants answers—which he deserves—but I just need a minute to collect myself. Every time I open my mouth to tell him it's like my throat closes and refuses to let the words pass. It's not that I'm afraid to tell him; I'm just worried what his reaction will be. He may say he doesn't blame me, but there's a dreadful fear in the back of my mind that he will. What if this ruins whatever connection we've created?

I glance over at him from the corner of my eye and see his jaw clenched tight, his knuckles gripping the steering wheel so hard they're starting to turn white. Despite the air feeling like it's getting sucked out of the car from all the nervous energy, a smile tugs at my lips at the sheer willpower it's probably taking him not to demand to know what the text said. My smile fades and I sigh, knowing that it's time to stop stalling and put him out of his misery. I turn around to check on Emma, but she's fast asleep. Not that it would matter; she won't be able to understand what's happening anyway.

Taking a deep breath, I turn back around and twist in my seat to face Chase fully. "So … I got a text," I say, pausing to watch his reaction, "From Courtney," I add.

His voice is gruff as he answers, still refusing to look at me. "I assumed that."

"Right," I mumble with a gulp. "Um, it was actually a follow up text. She sent one earlier."

This time he whips his head to the side to look at me. "When?" he demands.

I wince. "This morning. While you were at the front desk," I say quietly.

He turns his attention back to the road and curses under his breath. "Alright. What did she say?"

I take a deep breath, preparing for the hard part. "Remember that diner we went to the other day?" I ask carefully.

"Uh-huh," he says slowly. I look down at my hands in my lap, trying not to fidget. "Tatum." His harsh tone has me looking up at him, giving away just how close he is to losing it.

I lift my hands up in a placating gesture and decide it's best to just rip the Band-Aid off, blurting out everything in one breath. "She texted me telling me that one of Adam's friends, Nick, was at an extended family member's funeral who apparently lived in the middle of nowhere and they had to drive a bit to get to the nearest airport. And, well, I guess they wanted to stop for dinner along the way." I pause, taking a deep breath and quickly glance over at him. He continues to stare at the road ahead, sitting ramrod straight. The only indication he heard me is the slight tic of his jaw.

"They, uh, seemed to have stopped at the same diner we were at. Courtney overheard him talking to Adam in the hallway at school this morning saying he thought he saw me there. Which is why she texted me so early. Apparently, he had talked with our waitress, and she told him my name was Tatum …" I trail off as I watch him, waiting to see what he'll say.

"You told her your name?" he hisses through gritted teeth.

"It was a reflex," I say guiltily.

Chase is silent for a few seconds before he slams his palm against the steering wheel. "Fuck," he grunts loudly.

As soon as the word leaves his mouth, we both turn back to look at Emma right as she lets out a high-pitched wail. I'm about to tell Chase to pull over so I can comfort her when I feel the car skid off the road onto the shoulder. I unbuckle my seatbelt and am out of the car as soon as Chase puts it in park. I round the hood to open the driver's side back door and slide in next to her. I don't want to risk taking her out of her car seat since we're in the middle of nowhere on the side of the road. So instead, I try to distract her, grabbing one of her favorite rattling toys on the seat next to her and wave it in front of her, the plastic clinking together. It takes about five minutes of whispering and entertaining her before she settles down. I reach out and wipe the tears that have fallen from her cheeks. Only once I make sure she's calm enough do I climb back into the front seat.

I shoot Chase the strictest look I can muster and he looks at me, remorse clouding his features. "I'm really sorry about that, Tatum," he mutters.

I fold my arms across my chest, but I don't really blame him. He has every right to be upset. I panicked, too, when I first saw Courtney's text. I guess I was just better at internalizing my freak-out. Sighing, I uncross my arms and glance at him again. "It's okay, I get it. I sort of freaked out too," I hesitate before adding, "and I may have been a little nervous to tell you."

This time *he* gives *me* a stern look. "You should have told me right away."

"I know, I know. I'm sorry I didn't."

He swipes his hand down his face. "It's fine. Alright, what else did she say?"

"That was the first text. The one she just sent said that she was able to corner Nick without raising suspicion to ask him about it. He told her that Adam denied it was me. But there's no way to tell if Nick believed what Adam said or what Adam's going to do with this information." I worry my lip between my teeth. Adam has nothing to gain by finding me; it only makes his life more complicated.

My heart rate picks up at the realization that we might actually get caught by Nick freaking Ambrose. I just hope that we've covered our tracks well enough for that not to happen.

"That's it?" His voice startles me, but I nod at his question.

"Pretty much. She said she would keep us updated if she hears anything else. Since she's technically not supposed to know about Emma and no one really knows that we're friends, it'll be hard for her to stay on top of it. Especially with my parents."

He nods, understanding what I'm not saying. Right now, we're in a guessing game of not knowing what will come next. I may have been slightly naïve before, but now the fear of truly being on the run is getting to me.

"Well, the good news is we have a full day's head start. We just have to put as much distance between us and that diner as we can," I tell him, trying to stay positive.

He pinches the bridge of his nose with his index finger and thumb and inhales loudly through his nose. Wordlessly he drops his hand and reaches across me, his arm brushing up against my leg, leaving goosebumps along the exposed skin in its wake, and opens the glove compartment. He pulls out the map we've been using and studies it intently, his eyes scanning the page repeatedly. I guess that's one of the advantages of traveling without a clear destination—it makes it harder for my parents to find us. At least, I hope.

"Okay, what about this?" he finally says, interrupting my thoughts. I look over to where he's pointing. He runs his finger over the map as he's talking, showing me the outline of the route. "If we stay on the route we're on now, it basically dead-ends in Los Angeles. It looks like there are a ton of different highways that intersect it along the way, which would make it difficult for your parents to track where we go."

I nod my head in agreement, trusting his decision to keep us safe. "Where does that leave us then?" I ask.

He sways his head from side to side and purses his lips, weighing the different options. "If there's a place along the way that you like, we can stop there for a little bit and see how you like it. I was initially thinking of going all the way to California, but it's up to you." He shrugs nonchalantly, except the way he says it feels like there's more to it than he lets on. I narrow my eyes at him, debating whether I should push it or not, but when his pained eyes meet mine, I decide to drop it. It's been enough of a whirlwind morning; I don't want to add more to it than I already have.

"I'm sorry again for not telling you about the texts sooner," I say quietly instead.

"It's all good. We just need be more careful, at least until we're out of the woods, okay?"

"We will," I state firmly. It doesn't escape my notice that he said *we*, instead of putting the blame solely on me.

He nods back at me in agreement and hands me the map. He flips on the left turn signal and gets back onto the main road. I reach over to the dial and turn the radio on, letting some country bop fill the void. It fades into background noise as I look out the window, my mind drifting back to what Chase said. A small part of me—okay, maybe a big part—wants to know why he never came back to visit his dad. I feel like there's more to the story than him just casually mentioning California. I've never been to California—too many hippies, according to my parents—and I start wondering what it might be like. Will Emma and I live by the beach or up in the mountains? And, more importantly, will Chase stay close by, or will he leave us entirely?

I'm so engrossed in my daydreaming about California that I jump a little when I hear Chase's voice. He flashes me a grin, clearly trying to hold back his laughter. "Sorry, didn't mean to startle you."

I smile sheepishly at him, my cheeks flushed with embarrassment. "It's okay. I was just lost in my head."

His smile slowly drops from his face, and he clears his throat. "I've been thinking. You need to dye your hair," he says matter-of-factly.

I stare at him, my mouth agape. "Excuse me?"

"Your hair." He points towards my hair to emphasize his point. "You need to change the color of it. If your parents have hired people to look for you, then they're going to be looking for a blonde girl. I mean, that Nick guy easily recognized you, even with a cap on."

"Well yeah, but …" I trail off because I realize he's right. Nick thought he saw me and didn't hesitate to ask Adam about it. "Do I have to, though? Can't I just like, wear a wig or something?" I plead with him. I know I sound whiny even to my own ears, but I can't help it. Dyeing my hair is the last thing I want to do.

He shrugs. "I mean, you can. I just thought dyeing it would be a lot easier than wearing an itchy wig all the time. Besides, I don't even know where you would get one." He raises his brow at me questioningly.

I throw up my hands. "I don't know. Don't they have, like, stores in the mall for that?"

"A mall has a ton of security cameras though," he says, looking me over. "Yeah, not going to happen." I scrunch up my nose a little because, again, he's right.

I let out a loud groan and sink my head into my hands. "I've just never dyed my hair before." My voice comes out muffled behind my palms.

"It'll be okay, I promise," he says, but I hear the humor in his voice. I look up and narrow my eyes at him.

"You think this is funny, don't you." I state.

He laughs and looks at me, his smile fading into a smirk as he takes in my narrowed eyes and pursed lips. "No, I'm sorry, it's not funny. Just hard to imagine Tatum Rothchild with anything other than these golden locks everyone talks about." He reaches over and tugs on the end of my hair. I jerk out of his grip and his hand drops, his arm resting on the center console. His smile still in place.

"You've heard people talking about me?" I ask.

"Oh yeah. They told me about the princess in the castle with the long, beautiful blonde hair, just waiting to be rescued from the tower." His grin tugging at the corner of his lips lets me know he's joking, but I still feel the knot forming in my stomach.

"You have no idea," I mumble sourly.

He looks over and shoots me a quizzical look. "Want to talk about it?"

"Not really," I say, and the car is filled with a beat of awkward silence.

He taps his fingers against the steering wheel a few times before sitting up straighter. "I'm thinking you should go bright red." His words confuse me at first before I realize he's talking about my hair.

"Ugh, seriously. We're back to this?" I fold my arms across my chest and hit my head back against the headrest. I want to forget about the fact that I'll most likely be changing my hair color.

"Guess that's a no for red then. What about black? Brown? Maybe an auburn," he says with a smirk on his face.

I give him a deadpan look. He holds up his hands in a placating gesture. "Alright, I just figured you'd want to stick with neutrals, but we can work with colors. Are you a purple girl? No, that's not it. Hmm, blue? Oh yeah, definitely blue."

My lips quirk, but I still give him a stony expression. "That's a hard no for me."

"Yeah, you're probably right. You'd look better as a redhead anyway."

I gape at him, completely stunned by his declaration. Chase

waits a beat before a laugh escapes him. "Um …" is all I manage to say, my cheeks on fire. *Is … is he flirting with me?*

I smile, and soon I'm laughing along with him too. As our laughter fades, a comfortable silence fills the car. I feel lighter than I did just a few minutes ago and I guess I have him to thank for that. For momentarily distracting me, however brief it might be.

He glances at me. "Sorry if that was too far, I just wanted to cheer you up. And I am sorry you're having to do this. I'm not trying to downplay the situation you're in, but we really do need to be careful from now on." A serious expression crosses his face as he says, "It's just … if we get caught, I could end up going to jail for kidnapping, you know? If that's how your parents wanted to spin it. I'm nearly twenty, you're seventeen; the outcome doesn't exactly look too good for me."

I swallow over the lump in my throat, knowing that he's right. He's risking it all to ensure that Emma and I have a better future. I cast my eyes downward and stare at my lap, feeling like a child who's been scolded. "You're right, I'm sorry. I'll do what needs to be done."

He glances over at me. "Don't be sorry, I want to help you. I knew what I was getting into. It's just, we need to be more careful going forward," he says earnestly.

I nod. "Yeah, okay." He accepts my answer and looks back at the road, but something nags at me. I turn to face him. "Why *are* you helping me then? You just said you're taking a huge risk, so why do it at all?" I watch as he goes still at my question, and I tilt my head. "It's more than just the money, isn't it?"

His knuckles tighten on the steering wheel and I can tell he doesn't want to answer my question. "I wanted to help you," he says adamantly. "I *want* to help you. And yeah, having the money to get away was pretty nice."

I shake my head. "It doesn't have anything to do with your dad, then?"

He grinds his jaw. "I don't know what you're talking about."

I narrow my eyes at him, but I can tell by his stiff posture and the hard set of his jaw that this conversation is over.

About an hour later, we spot a drug store on the corner of the town we're passing through. We decide to stop there and see if we can get any hair dye.

"I can run in and grab it. Do you have a color in mind, or do you want me to pick?"

I bite my lip, and he briefly glances down at my mouth to where my lip is caught in between my teeth before shooting his eyes back to mine. My breath hitches and I try to quickly cover it up. "Uh, you pick. I'm too nervous."

He nods. "Alright." He gets out of the car, but stops once he's outside and bends down to look at me through the open door. "I promise I won't go bright red," he says in a playful tone, shooting me a wink. Then he straightens and shuts the car door.

I gape at him, unsure of what to do. I've never seen this side of him, and I'm too stunned at first to notice how my heart starts beating faster. "Gee, thanks," I mumble sarcastically into the empty space once my brain gets back on track.

I start chewing on my nail and try to focus on anything other than what color Chase could be picking out right now. I trust him enough by now to know that he won't actually pick out some crazy color. At least, I hope he won't. My knee is bouncing uncontrollably by the time he comes back to the car with a plastic bag in his hand. I grab it from him as soon as he gets in, and peek into the bag to see what color my new identity will be. On the box is a picture of a beautiful young woman sporting long, chestnut locks.

"So, brunette huh?" I raise my eyebrow at him.

He shrugs without looking at me. "Thought it would suit you."

I sigh. "Well, here's to hoping it looks good." I hold up the box in a fake salute.

I fiddle with the box in my hand as the silence becomes too

much. I know I told myself I would let it go, but I suddenly have this strong urge to get to know him more. Except I have a feeling that the only way I'll get answers from him is if I open up to him first. Even though I really don't want to rehash everything that has happened over the last year, I realize it's the only option I have. Taking a deep breath, I prepare myself for what I'm about to share.

"My parents were never really parents." I start to say, pausing when I notice him glance over at me. "I mean, they provided me with anything I could ever want. I lived in a big house, had all the latest fashion trends according to my mother, and went to the best school. But they weren't *really* parents. I felt like a puppet to them, someone they could show off to their friends." I scoff and shake my head. "It's kind of ironic, actually. They tried so hard to have a baby, yet when they had me, it seemed like they didn't care at all. It's like she got pregnant just because she wanted to check off a 'what you're supposed to do' list and called it a day."

Chase seems to sense where this is coming from, for what he said about the princess in the tower waiting to be rescued, because a guilty expression crosses his face. "I'm sorry, Tatum, for what I said earlier. I didn't mean anything—"

"No, it's fine." I cut him off with a wave of my hand. "You were right in a way; I did feel trapped. The only people who really knew me, knew how I felt, were Courtney and Adam. Everyone else just saw me as another girl with the perfect life." I think back to the type of person I was, of how much I was hiding myself to just blend in. Then I realize how much I've changed in such a short amount of time. It's also why Adam's decision hurt me as much as it did, because I thought he knew the real me better than anyone else. "And I think, in a way, I did want to be that person. Like maybe if I pleased my parents and everyone else around me enough, then there wouldn't be anything people could hold against me."

"I'm guessing getting pregnant wasn't just a way to get back at your parents then?" he asks jokingly.

I snort. "No, definitely not." I didn't realize how much lighter I'd feel by talking about this and I wonder if he can sense that I need him to take some of the seriousness out of this conversation. "No, they were beyond pissed when I finally told them."

"What happened?" he asks curiously, like he really does want to know.

I sigh, remembering their reaction. "They wanted me to get an abortion right away …until they found out that I had waited too long to tell them, and it wasn't an option at that point."

"Oh wow," he breathes.

I shrug. "I think part of me was in denial at first, hoping that it wasn't real. The other part knew what their response would be, and deep down I knew I didn't want that. I didn't really want to be a teen mom, but a bigger part of me didn't want to go through with an abortion. So, yeah, my mother didn't talk to me for a few weeks after that and my father still hasn't. I'm talking zero communication. He's even refused to be in the same room as me," I add.

His face has a red tint to it as he grinds out his next question. "Did Adam know?"

I nod my head. "Yeah, I told him a week after I found out." I glance at him out of the corner of my eye. "Like I said, I may have been in a little denial." He meets my gaze with understanding but doesn't say anything, letting me continue at my own pace.

"He didn't believe me at first—not until I showed him the four test results I had taken with him there. I was scared, and I could tell he was too, but I thought he'd be my rock through it all. He had been there for me until that point, helping me navigate the lifestyle our parents wanted for us. At the time, I thought we'd get through it together." I pause to wipe away a stray tear that has started to fall.

"Anyway, I was able hide my pregnancy in the beginning since it was winter in Connecticut. Then, after the holidays, my mother made up some elaborate excuse about how I was away in France, modeling and taking a 'sabbatical' from school—her words, not mine," I clarify. "No one except Courtney and Adam knew that I was really stuck sitting at home that whole time."

He looks at me with wide eyes. "They didn't let you leave at all?"

I shake my head. "Nope. They were too afraid someone would see me. Adam would visit occasionally, but eventually, said it would look weird if he was over all the time if I was supposedly in France, so he stopped coming by." I shrug as if doesn't bother me, but it does. I remember when he would come over; how he could never look me in the eye and never stayed over too long. "It made sense to me at the time, but now I realize it was because he knew what our parents were planning."

"What an asshole," Chase hisses through gritted teeth.

I let out a surprised laugh at that. "Yeah, well, you're not wrong."

He shakes his head in disgust. "He should have been there for you and for Emma. He should have manned up and done the right thing." His grip on the steering wheel tightens, hatred coating his every word.

"It's funny; I really did think he was there for me at first. But looking back, knowing he was aware of our parents' plan the whole time, I realize he was just waiting for it all to be over. Keeping me placated long enough until I signed the papers, and he wasn't on the hook for being a parent anymore."

"He's a piece of shit, Tatum," he growls.

I gently rest my hand on his arm. "It's okay, I'm fine," I say, trying to reassure him. "Surprisingly, I'm glad things turned out the way they did. This situation showed me Adam's true colors, how he isn't someone I can really count on. Now, I'm getting the opportunity to learn how to count on myself. And that's a good thing. I'd much rather be on the run with you than stuck in a position that's not the best for me or Emma."

He looks over and locks eyes with me. It only lasts a few seconds, but something flares to life behind his blue eyes, igniting a spark between us that hasn't been there before. The moment passes as fast as it appears, and I'm suddenly acutely aware of the fact that my hand is still resting on his bicep. I quickly pull it back as if it burned me.

"I just mean that you've been very helpful, and I'm grateful that you offered to help us out."

He shakes his head quickly, as if he's trying to clear his thoughts. "Right. Of course."

I self-consciously clear my throat. "Moral of the story is don't have sucky parents and don't let your boyfriend convince you not to use protection," I say weakly, hoping a joke will ease the tension. It falls flat, though, and seems to only make Chase angry again. His breaths come out in short puffs, his nostrils flaring on each exhale. After a particularly long exhale, his shoulders slump and he relaxes back into his seat.

"I'm sorry you had to deal with that. It's not fair to you or Emma," he says.

My cheeks redden with the realization that I just told him everything. "Thanks. And thanks for listening to me. It's nice to talk about this with someone else."

"Anytime." He looks over to me with a smile and I swear butterflies erupt in my belly. I don't know where these feelings are coming from, but they need to stop. Like right now. Emma and I have already had one guy disappoint us; I don't want another one to as well.

The car ride is surprisingly peaceful after that. Given what I told him, I thought there might be a strain in the car, but it's the opposite. We stop a few times so I can feed Emma and change her diaper while Chase and I make idle chitchat. There aren't any more deep conversations like before, but there is a comradery between us that hasn't been there before.

"It looks like there's a motel about ten miles up ahead," Chase says, nodding to a sign on the side of the road. It's slightly hidden in the trees but I can see the bold letters spell out, *Goldview Lodge – 10 miles*, with a bright, red arrow pointing down to a cardboard cutout building that looks like a log cabin. "You about ready to stop or do you think we should keep going?"

I shake my head. "No, let's stop. Besides," I smile over at him sarcastically. "I still have to dye my hair, remember?"

He smirks right back at me. "How could I forget?"

I roll my eyes and exactly thirteen minutes later we pull up outside of a motel that looks as realistic to a log cabin in real life as it did in the picture. We check in and despite what I might've thought, the room ends up having a cozy feel to it. The beds have flannel coverings on top of them and the lamps have a bunch of antlers glued together at the base. There are pictures of deer in the woods on the walls, while green checkered curtains frame the window. The only thing missing is a fireplace or else I would've believed we had somehow ended up in a real cabin in the woods.

I take Emma out of her car seat and hold her in my arms as Chase walks to the bathroom. "I need to give Emma a quick bath," I say when he puts the box of dye on the bathroom counter.

He turns his head and smirks at me. "You wouldn't be stalling, would you, Tatum?"

I flush. "Nope. Not at all. This is all for Emma."

"Uh-huh," he says with a smile in his voice. My cheeks are pink, and I walk into the bathroom to stand next to him. "Take your time." He glances down at Emma before he turns and walks away, leaving us alone in the bathroom.

I get Emma undressed and grab a washcloth from the towel

rack. I wait until the water is warm enough and duck the washcloth underneath it, pouring some of her soap onto it. I clean her and grab the other damp washcloth to wipe the soap off. Once I'm finished, I leave the bathroom and find Chase lounging on the bed, flipping through channels on the old TV. I put a diaper on Emma followed by her onesie and lay her down in her crib that Chase has already set up for me.

Chase mutes the tv and raises an eyebrow at me, but I ignore his stare. I grab one of my old, oversized T-shirts that I packed, and go to the bathroom to put it on. Even though I've never dyed my hair, I assume it'll be messy.

I rip open the box, dumping its contents on the counter. I grab the instructions and read through them a few times. It seems simple enough, so I pick up the bottle labeled "2", pour it into the bottle labeled "1", and shake it up. The white base starts to turn brown as the contents mix. I hesitate and swallow roughly. I stare down at the bottle, trying to find the courage to go through with this. A hand reaches out and I startle, glancing over to see Chase putting on the clear latex gloves.

"What are you doing?" I ask him.

He looks in the mirror and catches my eye in our reflection. "Helping you dye your hair," he states matter-of-factly.

"But, huh?" I stammer, squinting at him. "Getting the dye was more than enough help, and I'm perfectly capable of dyeing it myself."

"I know that. But you've also been standing there just staring at it for five minutes," he says.

"Have not," I say, but I know that's a lie.

He shrugs and starts to remove the glove, peeling it off one finger at a time. "Suit yourself."

"Wait, wait." I falter. He pauses his movements, the glove still hanging off his hand, and peers down at me. I take a deep breath, letting the air gust out of my lungs on my exhale. "You can help me," I tell him. It's not like I'm thrilled about this whole situation to begin with, but I might as well let him help.

Chase nods his head and slips his glove back on. He picks up the bottle and flattens down the top of my hair, tilting my head just a bit. I cringe slightly when the first drop of cool liquid hits my scalp. He pulls the color down through the strands of my hair with his fingers and then repeats the process underneath, parting my hair each time. By the time he's gotten halfway down my head, it no longer seems as daunting. Chase works in silence and it feels like an oddly intimate gesture, having him do this for me. He's so close to me that I can feel his breath fanning the back of my neck.

"Okay, I think I got everything," he tells me, putting the bottle back on the counter.

"Super," I mumble. Avoiding looking in the mirror, I grab the instructions and double-check the amount of time I need to wait before I can wash it out. Twenty minutes.

I turn around and lean against the counter, folding my arms over my chest. "So, uh, thanks for doing this." I point to my wet hair.

He smiles over at me. "No big deal."

Chase rips the gloves off and throws them in the trash can under the sink. I stare down at the brown color that coats the once clear gloves and scowl at it. My hands itch to reach up and grab a strand of my hair to look at the color, so I shove them under my armpits instead.

"What do you want to do once we reach California?" Chase asks, and I jerk my head over to look at him, finding him sitting down on the bed closest to me. My bed. I didn't even hear him leave the bathroom. His posture is relaxed, but his eyes study me intently. I shift uncomfortably, both at the thought of him on my bed and at the way he watches me through his lashes.

"What?"

"When we get to California," he clarifies as if I didn't hear him the first time. "Do you want to go to school, get a job ... anything?"

I push off the counter and walk over to him, his eyes trailing my every move, and slump down beside him. I mull over his question before shrugging. "I guess I haven't really given it much thought."

"Fair enough. This did all happen kind of fast," he quips. "The only plan I have is to work at a garage and someday open my own." I smile faintly at him before staring straight ahead and collecting my thoughts.

I nod with a newfound confidence. "I want to get my GED," I finally say. "Then maybe I can work part-time somewhere while I get my degree. It just depends on where Emma and I end up and if I can find someone to watch her. But I don't know, I can always get a degree online, too." I sigh and bite my lip, trying to think it over. I'm lost in my thoughts, but I see his slight nod, seeming satisfied by my answer. "What about you?" I ask.

He looks at me confused. "What about me?"

I shrug nonchalantly. "Are you planning on staying in California as well or are you going to head somewhere else?" I wait on bated breath for his answer.

After a moment he finally answers. "I'm staying in California."

The breath I was holding whooshes from my lungs; I didn't expect him to say that. "O—okay." I stutter and clear my throat. I'm relieved when my voice comes out even. "Any particular reason why?"

I can feel him look over at me, really look at me, but I don't meet his gaze. He stares at the side of my face as he seems to contemplate how he wants to answer me. I squirm restlessly and before I can think better of it, I glance up at him. We lock eyes and whatever he sees must pacify him. He turns back and looks straight ahead as he answers me. "My mom grew up there."

"Oh." I blink. Courtney never really told me much about his mom—although, it's not like I've ever really asked either.

"I'm assuming Courtney hasn't told you anything about her, has she?"

I blush ruefully and shake my head. "Um, no, not really."

He nods as if he knew this all along. "I figured. There's a lot of drama with our dad—a lot that Courtney doesn't even know—and it's partly why I only visited that one time." He trails off, seemingly lost in thought. I never had a ton of conversations with their dad, but he seemed pretty nice to me. "Anyway, my mom passed away a few months ago from cancer. That's the reason why I've been living with my dad; I had too many medical bills I needed to pay."

I suck in a sharp breath and gently place my hand on top of his. "I'm so sorry, Chase."

He glances down to where my hand is covering his but doesn't make a move to pull it away. "It's okay." He looks up at me and his eyes are slightly misty. "Which is why your offer was too good to refuse."

Understanding suddenly dawns on me. "The money," I state.

He nods. "Mostly that, yeah. But also to get away from my dad."

"Was he really that bad?" I ask carefully.

"To me, he was," he says.

"What happened?" I whisper. I didn't notice it at first, but as we've been talking, I've gradually started shifting closer to him. I glance down and discover my leg is almost touching his. This is the most he's shared with me, and I find myself hanging on every word, wanting to know more.

He thinks it over for a moment, but instead of answering me, he slides his hand out from under mine. Patting my leg, the one that's practically touching his, he says, "That's a story for another day." He then gets up and walks over to the sink. I watch as he rummages through the box of hair dye and pulls out two small bottles labeled shampoo and conditioner. "Come on, Goldilocks, it's time to wash that color out."

I squint in confusion. "How'd you know it was time?"

He points to the clock on the table between the two beds, and I follow his gaze. Sure enough, twenty minutes have gone by. "I've been watching."

I look back at him. "You distracted me?" It comes out like a question, even though I know that's exactly what he did.

"Got you to stop obsessing over your hair, didn't it?" He smirks at me and sets the bottles down on the counter. I shake my head because he's right—it did.

CHAPTER 8

I stare back at my reflection through the thick layer of dust that coats the grimy gas station bathroom mirror. It's been two days since I dyed my hair, and I still don't know how I feel about it. I've only washed it once, which means the color hasn't faded, but it's still weird to look at. The more I look at it, the more I realize it's not as awful as I first thought it would be. I lift my hand to run my fingers through my hair—something I've been doing constantly since dyeing it—only to stop short and remember I can't because my hands are still dirty. Which is the reason I came in here in the first place. I sigh and drop my hand, cringing when it accidentally brushes against the dirty countertop. It's not like I can wash my hands, because the rusty sink doesn't actually work. And I tried—several times. I should probably invest in a gallon-sized bucket of hand sanitizer so I can avoid these types of bathrooms next time.

I check the paper towel dispenser, but it's empty as well. Sighing again, I crumple up a piece of toilet paper and wipe off my hands the best I can. I glance back at my reflection in the mirror one last time, still not used to the person looking back at me. Shaking my head, I exit the bathroom. I head to the aisle with hand sanitizers and grab a few small bottles. As I walk up to the counter, I can't resist stopping to grab a bag of Twizzlers, too.

"This all?" An older woman with a smoker's cough and lots of wrinkles around her face asks when I put my items on the counter.

"Yeah."

After I pay, I grab the bag with my purchases in it and mumble a quick, "Thank you." I don't get anything in response, but I didn't expect to. I walk across the lot and around the side of the building to where Chase parked the car.

"All good?" Chase asks when I get in the car.

"Yeah, but it was gross," I say with a shudder.

I reach into the bag and pull out one of the bottles of hand sanitizer. I squirt a generous amount onto my hands and rub them together frantically, making sure to get all the germs off. Chase leans over and peers into the bag. "I knew it," he says.

I shoot him a confused stare, still rubbing my hands together. "Knew what?"

Reaching down he sticks his hand in the bag and pulls out the jumbo pack of Twizzlers I bought. He gives me a smug smile and I roll my eyes. "Oh whatever."

"You just couldn't resist, could you?"

"Nope," I say as I snatch the bag back.

He lets out a low chuckle and shifts the car in gear, leaving the rundown gas station behind us as we get back on the road again. "I'll be so happy once we're back in civilization."

He looks over at me, darts his eye to the rearview mirror, then looks back at me again, before returning his focus to the road. "You do realize that we just stopped at a gas station with an actual person working there, right?"

I shake my head at him. "I know that. I just meant when there's more than one dirty old gas station for, like, a hundred miles. I'm tired of looking at nothing but fields, dirt, and mountains."

He nods. "So, you could never live out west. Noted," he chuckles.

I stare out the window, the radio playing softly in the background, and sigh loudly. "Okay, I think I may be a little bored." I look at him, and he tilts his head, contemplating something.

After a moment he looks back at me. "Want to play a game?"

I perk up, intrigued. "Like what?"

He thinks for a moment, pursing his lips slightly. "Actually, I don't know. The only game I've played in the car has been I Spy."

"Oh! I used to play that game when I was little, on our drives out to the Hamptons. Well, a version of that game ... and I would play it by myself. Basically, I would randomly pick a color—the first one I could think of—and then name as many things as I could see in that color." I drift off and cast my eyes downward, realizing now how sad that is. "My parents never wanted to play that game with me, but it was the only thing I wanted to do. Surprisingly, it was actually pretty fun."

"Alright, let's play it then," he says, and I appreciate him doing this for me without acknowledging the sadness in my voice. He looks out around, studying our surroundings, and I do the same. Considering there's not much around us, I'm pretty sure this will be a quick game. After a minute, he says, "I spy something ... orange."

I glance around and a smile takes over my face. I turn around to confirm my guess before saying, "Emma's giraffe."

He nods in confirmation. "Yup. Your turn."

"I spy something ... yellow?" It comes out sounding more like a question and I cringe inwardly.

He laughs but thankfully doesn't call me out on it. "The line in the road."

"Too easy," I tease him, like I wasn't the one who asked it.

"Okay, then. I spy something green."

"That tree over there." He nods again, and suddenly, I'm over this game. It makes me feel like that little kid again—the one whose parents wouldn't even play a simple game with her. An overwhelming sense of panic washes over me, and before I realize what I'm doing, I ruin the game for us.

"My turn, hmm, let's see. I spy something brown. Oh! The dirt," I say before he even has a chance to answer. I know I'm being rude, but I can't seem to stop myself. "I'll go again. Something black: the road. Something yellow again: that sign we just passed for some animal crossing. Oh, look at that, game's over." I lift my hands up in the air in a *what can you do* gesture. "There's literally nothing out here!" I exclaim in exasperation.

He looks slightly annoyed at my outburst. "Well shit, Tatum, there's not a lot of options for games." I sulk down in my seat knowing he's right. I'm about to suggest that we go back to silence when he surprises me. "What about twenty questions or something?"

A slow smile spreads across my face. Now we're getting somewhere. "I thought you didn't want to play that game. The whole 'there's no reason to get to know each other' thing?"

His hands tighten on the steering wheel, but he doesn't disagree with me. "Do you want to play or not?" he asks tersely.

I raise my hands up in a placating gesture before dropping them back in my lap. "Alright, alright. I'll go first." I have a lot of questions I want to ask, but instead, I blurt out the first, most typical one I can think of. "What's your favorite color?"

He glances at me, probably not expecting me to ask him that. "Red," he answers hesitantly. "What about you?"

"Is that your question?" I ask. He nods, avoiding my gaze. "Blue. See, that wasn't so hard, was it?" I say gleefully.

He rolls his eyes. "Just eat your Twizzlers and ask another question."

I smile at him as I rip open the pack and devour a strawberry rope of goodness. "What's your all-time favorite band?"

"I don't listen to a lot of music, but I do like Maroon 5." I look at him with raised eyebrows and he shrugs, "I like having them on in the background when I'm working on cars," he says.

"Huh. Didn't see that one."

"Oh, okay, wise guy. What's yours?"

"Taylor Swift, obviously," I say with a smirk.

He laughs. "Of course it is."

"Hey, she may be basic to some people, but so is water, and you still need that to survive."

He looks at me and shakes his head with a laugh. "You're a little weird, you know that?"

I smile proudly at him. "Thank you."

"Your turn then."

"Alright. What's your favorite food?"

"Italian. Favorite ice cream?" he asks without missing a beat.

"Ooh, rocky road." I grab another Twizzler and chew on it while I think about what else to ask him. "Favorite movie?"

"*Breakfast Club.*"

He says it immediately with such a straight face that I let out a very unattractive snort before I start laughing. I'm laughing hard, almost gasping for air, when I ask him, "Are you serious?"

He smirks and reaches over, lightly flicking my arm. "Hey, it's my turn to ask the question." He smiles at me teasingly. "Favorite book?"

I roll my eyes at his avoidance of my question, deciding to let him have that little bit be a mystery, and wave him off. "Easy. *The Great Gatsby.*"

"Really?" he asks, sounding bemused.

I stick my tongue out at him. "My turn to ask questions, remember?"

He shakes his head at me. His posture is relaxed as he sits back in his seat, keeping one hand on the steering wheel, the other one resting on the center console.

"Hmm ... favorite animal?"

"Tiger."

"Interesting," I say slowly.

"What's your favorite holiday?"

"Definitely Christmas." I've always loved Christmas. Not because of the presents—well not *all* because of the presents—but because I love everything about the holiday. The hot chocolate, the Christmas tree, the lights, and the snow; it makes everything feel happier somehow. It was the only time I actually enjoyed going to one of the countless social events my parents dragged me to, being surrounded by all the holiday magic.

Knowing it's my turn, I blurt out a question I've always wanted to ask someone. "If you could spend the day with any person, dead or alive, who would it be?"

He gets quiet, contemplating for a moment, before he replies. "Probably my mom," he says sadly. Suddenly, it feels like all the air has been sucked out of the car. He says it so longingly that my heart hurts for him.

It doesn't feel like we're playing this lighthearted game anymore. I ask softly, "What was she like?"

He smiles thoughtfully, "She was the best. Life dealt her some pretty rough cards, but she still managed to make my childhood fun. I remember one year, when I was about ten or eleven, we didn't have a lot of money for Christmas presents. Instead of getting me something, she asked me what the *one* thing I wanted to do was, and we would spend the whole day doing just that." He scoffs at a memory, "I don't even remember why I said it now, but I told her I wanted to eat turkey sandwiches with cranberry sauce and throw a football in the park."

My cheeks hurt from smiling as I listen to him remembering these moments with her. "And that's what we did for the entire day. She packed a huge cooler full of different turkey sandwiches and snacks—some with cranberry sauces, others with mac n cheese. I think one even had gravy on it." He laughs and shakes his head, lost in his own little world of grief and remembrance. "We sat underneath a huge oak tree and ate all the sandwiches, trying out the different combinations. She wasn't the most coordinated, but damn did she try her best to throw the football for me. I think we ended up just tossing it back and forth for hours, and not once did she complain. I was exhausted by the end of it, but I was having so much fun I didn't want the day to end. That's one of my favorite memories."

I place my hand on top of his on the console, just like I had in the motel. "That sounds like a great day," I say sadly.

He looks over and gives me a small smile. "It really was."

We stare at each other for a few seconds, and I feel like I've seen a whole new side of Chase. He hasn't been nearly as closed off and cold to me lately, but talking about his mom has really softened a part of him. In this moment, I realize that I don't want to say goodbye to him when we get to California. He's starting to burrow his way into my heart and I find myself wanting to comfort him, to know every detail of his life, and find out his likes and dislikes.

"What about you? What's your favorite memory?" he asks, pulling me from my thoughts, as though we're back to playing the game. I hadn't even noticed that he turned back to the road; I was so lost in my own head. I pull my hand away from his, suddenly feeling awkward, like the moment we just shared is gone. I think about his question, and I wish there was one that came to mind right away—one memory that I could revisit again and again, to remember the way it felt, just like he did. But the truth is, there isn't a single memory that I can think of.

"I don't think I have a favorite memory," I mumble more to myself than to him.

"Really? None at all?"

My mind instantly wanders back to the very first time I met Chase. Courtney and I were lounging on her pool chairs when he came running across the deck and cannonballed into the pool, splashing water everywhere. Courtney had cried out, complaining about how he splashed her with water, but I couldn't take my eyes off him. Thankfully, I had on big-framed sunglasses that covered half my face so he couldn't see me staring at him. He had just pushed back his brown, shaggy, wet hair when his sparkling blue eyes swung to mine, causing a jolt deep in the pit of my stomach. He had titled his head to the side and asked who I was, all while keeping his gaze locked on me.

I felt nervous and flustered for some reason when Courtney told him my name. I was too tense to say it myself, in case it came out high and squeaky. This way, at least, I could pretend to be mysterious. Instead of asking me any questions, or better yet, telling me I was the coolest girl he's ever met, he just said "hey" and dove right back into the pool. At the time, I had felt the tinge of disappointment, but quickly remembered Adam and realized I had no right to be. Yet, it's still a memory I'll never forget. Of course, I can't tell him that, though. So, I say the next best thing that comes to mind.

"Honestly? Probably this moment right here. Knowing Emma's safe with me and finding the courage to leave everything behind in order to do what's best for her. Being able to learn who I am and who I want to be. So, yeah, this will probably be my favorite memory."

"What about Emma's birth?"

I get why he's asking me that, because it's valid. It should've been one of my happiest memories; the day I brought her into this world. But all I do is shake my head because I know it's one I wouldn't want to relive. "Besides the fact that I was in pain for hours?" I snort. "That's one thing they don't tell you about the miracle of birth. But no, as happy as I am that she's here now, her birth wasn't the best."

"Why not?" he asks intently.

I sigh, knowing he probably won't like my answer. "I was all alone for it. My parents didn't want me going to the hospital and having any record of it, so they forced me to do a home birth. Everything was still fragile at the time, so I went along with what they wanted. But then my mother ended up not even being there for it, claiming she had a weak stomach, and Adam had school. It was just a few nurses my parents hired discreetly there to help me."

As I guessed, Chase looks immensely angry. "Pieces of shit. Not that I thought they were winning people to begin with, but still."

I shrug. "I'm used to it, I guess. Plus, it was kind of better that none of them were there with me because it made me realize that I would do anything for Emma. It was me and her against the world from the very beginning."

Chase can't let it go, though; he just shakes his head like he didn't hear a word of what I just said. "I thought my dad was an asshole, but your parents are real pieces of work."

"Chase, what happened with your dad?" I ask, partly because I see my opportunity and I want to take it, but also because I *really* want to change the subject.

I can tell he's so caught up from talking about his mom and me telling him about my parents, because he doesn't even hesitate. "I guess it started when—" Just as I'm about to do an internal victory dance, Emma lets out a high-pitched wail, interrupting whatever Chase was about to say.

As soon as I hear her wail, I immediately know what's wrong. "Oh my gosh, I totally forgot to give her a bottle when we stopped last."

Chase is already pulling over to the side of the road by the time I finish talking. I don't even have time to feel guilty about the fact that I forgot to feed her as I hop out of the car and slide into the backseat. I need to figure out what to do first—make her a bottle or comfort her? Chase must have read my mind during my two-second internal debate because he's already out of the car as well.

"I'll get the bottle ready while you hold her."

I don't think twice as I start unbuckling Emma. "Thank you," I say, relieved.

I get her out of the car seat and hold her against my chest, lightly bouncing her up and down in my arms. It seems to do the trick because her cries begin to taper off. Chase quickly mixes up the formula and hands me the bottle to feed her. I readjust her in my arms and put the bottle to her lips. As she starts drinking the milk, I look up at Chase, hoping to convey with my eyes just how thankful I am that he stepped up to help me. He nods in understanding and waits just outside the car while I continue to feed her.

She must have been really hungry because she guzzles down the milk in record time. Chase reaches over and hands me a burp cloth I didn't notice he had. I sit her up on my lap and pat her back until she burps. A few dribbles of saliva run down her chin onto the cloth, and I wipe it away until she's clean. Once I know she's okay again, I put her back into her car seat and buckle her in. Chase waits until I've rounded the car before he moves to open his door. We climb in simultaneously, but I'm distracted as I'm putting on my seatbelt. The guilt over forgetting to feed her starts to gnaw at me. I worry my lip between my teeth as I think about how I was too distracted earlier to remember, and then only fed her once she was crying out for it. I'm so lost in my guilt that I don't notice Chase has already merged back onto the road.

"Don't do that."

"Do what?" I glance over at him, confused by what he said.

He points a finger in my direction. "I can see your mind turning, it's written all over your face. You think you're a bad mom because you forgot to feed her, but you can't do that."

I shrug weakly and hang my head a little. "I can't help it." I sigh in defeat and glance out the window.

"Tatum, look at me." He waits until I turn my head slightly, not entirely giving him my full attention, but enough to show I'm listening. He reaches over and puts his hand on my leg. I look down at it quickly before snapping my eyes to his face, watching his features as he tells me earnestly. "You're an amazing mom. Don't ever feel like you're not. What you're doing for Emma is incredible, and I can promise you that you aren't the only one who's done that before. All that matters is that Emma is happy and healthy, and has a mom like you; one who will do anything for her."

I feel my eyes watering with unshed tears by the time he's done talking. I try to speak, but a choked sob comes out instead, making me clear my throat a few times. "Thank you, Chase. That means a lot. I don't think anyone has ever told me that before; that I'm doing a good job. It's just hard sometimes." I sniffle and wipe my eyes before any of the tears can fall.

He gives me a sad smile. "I get it, but I'm also here to help you. I hope you know that." He squeezes my leg before removing his hand and resting it on the center console. My stomach flips at that, and suddenly I find myself wondering what it would be like if he didn't leave us when we got to California. How would it be if he decided to stay and continue helping me with Emma? I quickly shake off those unwelcome thoughts, knowing that's not a possibility. I'm just a means to an end for him, and he doesn't want to be strapped down with all these responsibilities that aren't his.

As the silence stretches on, I have a feeling the window of him opening up to me has closed. I don't mind too much, though. He talked about his mom more than I expected him to, and the moment to talk about his dad is over. I stare out at the vast landscape as we drive by, watching as dirt flies up in the wind around our car with the sun high in the sky above us. It's almost peaceful out here, being surrounded by nature.

"My mom was the other woman," Chase says suddenly, catching me off guard.

My eyes widen in surprise. "What?"

He looks over and studies me carefully. "I'm assuming Courtney never told you the full story?"

I shake my head no. Courtney never told me much about their past. All I knew was that she had a half-brother who was two years older than us.

He sighs and nods his head. "I figured as much. I'm not a hundred percent sure *she* even knows what all happened."

"She only talked about you that one summer you came to visit. I never really knew about you before then."

He swallows hard and his voice is rough. "Right. I was dreading that summer. It was the first time I was meeting his family and staying with them for two months."

"You weren't around much," I state.

"I tried not to be."

"So," I ask hesitantly. "Did your dad know about you before then?"

He nods. "Yup. He's known about me since I was born."

"Oh," I say, my eyes widening again. I try to school my features as quickly as I can. I know that couldn't have been easy for him, knowing his dad knew about him but not visiting him until he was fourteen.

"I know what you're thinking." He looks over, chuckling at me.

"No, I'm n—" I start to protest, but one pointed look from him tells me he's not buying it. "Okay, fine. Maybe I am," I concede.

He lets out a humorless laugh. "It's fine, I've made peace with it." He pauses for a minute before adding, "sort of."

"I'm sorry," I whisper. He peers over at me but doesn't say anything. "What happened then? I mean, between your mom and Courtney's parents?"

He shrugs. "I actually don't know. My mom never told me any details, but I assume it ended badly. I think that's why we ended up in Texas."

"Oh. I didn't realize you lived somewhere else."

"*Technically*, I was born in California, but I lived in Texas my whole life." I narrow my eyes at him, waiting for him to continue. He lets out a sigh and carries on. "My mom met my dad when she was a waitress out in California. He would come by to see her whenever he was in town on business. They had a very brief love affair that ended when she found out he was married. She was heartbroken—she really thought he was the love of her life. It was only a few weeks after she cut things off with him that she found out she was pregnant with me. She vowed that she would never keep me from him, but she would also never ask for anything from him either."

"Wow," I say. "That must have been hard for her."

He just shrugs. "At times it was. But like I said, she did her best to give me everything she could, so I never really felt like I was missing out."

"Yeah, but knowing that you're going to be a single mom while the man you love goes on to start his own family," I shake my head at him. "That had to be tough."

"Kind of like someone else I know." He smiles over at me and then pointedly looks back at Emma. I feel a blush start to crawl up my neck and I have no doubt that my cheeks are bright red by now.

"So, um," I clear my throat, wanting to get the focus off me and back to him, "is that why you have such a strained relationship with him, then?"

He lets out a humorless laugh. "Partly. It's also the fact that when I finally did get the courage to go visit him, all I felt was this *indifference* that I was there. I felt like I was this thorn in their side all summer long—a constant reminder of his infidelity. And then I felt guilty. Like it was my fault that he cheated," he says sarcastically, rolling his eyes at himself. "Of course, I didn't find out until later that the reason my mom encouraged me to go was because she was starting her cancer treatments that summer and didn't want me around for that."

"Oh wow. I'm sorry, Chase."

I look over and notice his eyes are glassy. My heart lurches in my chest and I want more than anything to reach out to him, but I keep my hands clasped firmly in my lap waiting for him to continue.

"That's the main reason why I hate him. When I told him she had cancer and how quickly it was spreading, he never came to visit her." He clears his throat a few times. "She thought this man was the love of her life and he didn't come. He didn't even call. The only thing he did was send us a few checks in the mail to pay for her treatment that mom tore up. She didn't want his help, and neither do I."

"Then why were you living with him?"

He lets out a deep sigh and shakes his head. "Because I had no money left. We spent almost everything we had trying to get her better. I missed out on going to school, spent most of my time driving her from clinic to clinic, but it was useless. After she died, my dad basically forced me to come back and live with him. He told me I could work and save up money by living there with him instead of trying to rent an apartment somewhere else. I didn't want to, but I needed the money enough to know not to be stubborn about it."

"And then Courtney came to you with my offer," I surmise.

He nods. "Like I said, it was too good to pass up."

I reach down and pick up the half empty water bottle lying on the floorboard. I lift it up high in a makeshift *cheers* to him. "Well, here's to California—to leaving our pasts behind us and forging a new and better future."

He lets out a full laugh and grabs his own water bottle from the center console to clink it against mine. "Cheers to that."

With a big smile on my face, I unscrew the cap and take a big swig of the water, savoring the moment. I glance at Chase and see him grinning as he takes his own sip of water. I know it wasn't easy for him to talk about that, but I'm really glad he did. I feel like I understand him so much better now and sense a friendship starting to form between us.

CHAPTER 9

Our trip continues over the next three days, and I've never been more ready to be out of the car and settled in one place, while simultaneously never wanting this to end. We've seen the mountains, the desert, the endless road; we've covered the south and most of the west. We've listened to all the different stations on the radio and eaten more fast food than I can handle. We've stopped at some of the dirtiest gas stations and stayed at some of the worst motels. Yet, somewhere along the way, we started making this trip less about getting to our destination and more about enjoying the little moments with each other. There's been no further word from Courtney, so we're still taking precautions, not out of the woods yet.

I try not to think about it too hard as I look down at the map. According to this, we should cross the border into California sometime tomorrow, making this our last stop for the night before we reach our destination. There's a bittersweet feeling surrounding me at that thought. This road trip has been nothing like I imagined. One thing that surprises me is that Chase gets a little souvenir for Emma at each place we stop at. My heart nearly burst out of my chest when he told me he does it so she'll always have a part of this trip with her. That when she grows older, she'll remember the journey and how she got there. My only fear is that this bubble we've created around ourselves will come crashing down, and I'm not sure how I'll feel when it does.

"I haven't seen a sign for a place to stop in at least thirty miles," Chase says.

I look up and see that he's right; there's nothing along the highway. The sun has already started to set, giving way to the darkness creeping up on us. I look back down at the map.

"It looks like there's a town coming up soon."

He nods his head in acknowledgment. "We'll just keep driving until we see a place."

"I'll have to feed Emma as soon as we get there. I forgot to get another water bottle for her when we stopped last."

He looks in the rear-view mirror at her. "Hopefully it won't be too much longer."

"Yeah, hopefully." I lean my head against the window and stare outside, watching and waiting for any sign to pop up.

It's an hour later when we finally reach the next town and see a sign for a place to stay in their 'Historic Downtown District'. I'm just relieved for a place at all because Emma was getting grumpier by the minute, and I wasn't sure how much longer we'd be able to make it. It's one of the larger small towns we've stayed in, evident by the old Victorian-styled hotel we see when we pull into the parking lot.

"Remember to keep your head down, just in case," Chase says as he shifts the car into park.

I nod, slightly annoyed because I know the drill, but he's already opening the car door and getting out, completely turned away from me. I huff an exasperated breath and get out of the car, too. I get Emma's car seat out and round the car to where Chase is waiting. He tugs his baseball cap down over his forehead with his free hand and nods for me to follow him. I roll my eyes but do as he asked, falling in step behind him. As we get near the entrance, the automatic doors a slide open to reveal a massive foyer. Directly in front of us is a round wooden table topped with a clear glass vase that holds an assortment of flowers about a foot tall. It's eye-level and momentarily blocks our view of the rest of the hotel. Underneath it lies a big, beautiful Parisian rug, and as we round the table, I'm able to take in the room fully.

The entire interior matches the exterior; a blend of the old Victorian style mixed with fragments of modern textures. There's a fireplace to the right of us with a low fire already burning, its flames casting a warm glow on the surrounding walls. Our shoes echo on the marbled tile floor as we walk, and when I look down, I notice there's gold splashes mixed within the surface. A massive chandelier hangs above us, catching my attention as the light from the fire reflects off the tiny crystals, complementing the black ceiling. Although, upon closer inspection, I see that it's not entirely black. It has shimmering dots all along it that glow, reminding me of a night sky. The whole lobby is a clash of color and decorations, but works in a way that feels both rich and cozy at the same time.

"Hey, head down."

I look and find Chase stopped in front of me. I hadn't realized I had been standing in the middle of the lobby, gazing up at the ceiling with my mouth hanging open slightly. I quickly snap it closed and lower my head down. "Shit, sorry," I mumble, feeling increasingly embarrassed at being caught staring at the ceiling.

Chase shakes his head as he turns and walks towards the front desk. I can't help but feel like I've been scolded again, and I'm ashamed of how annoyed I was with him just minutes earlier. He was right, once again, and I forgot to listen. My emotions are all over the place by the time I reach the front desk. I position myself halfway behind him, making sure that I'm somewhat hidden. A petite young blonde woman walks up behind the desk with a name tag that says Jessica. She greets us with a megawatt smile and her hand brushes a lock of her golden curls behind her ear that I'm immediately envious of.

"Hi there. Welcome to the Thatcher Hotel. Are you checking in?" she asks.

"Yeah, we don't have any reservations, but I was wondering if you have a room available. Two beds, please," Chase says in a polite voice.

Jessica nods and taps away on the keyboard before her, eyes scanning the computer screen. She winces slightly and looks up at us with polite regret. "I'm so sorry. Unfortunately, it seems that we're pretty full for tonight."

"Do you have any rooms available at all?" Chase asks almost pleadingly.

She looks back down at the computer screen. "Hmm, let me see." After a few clicks on the keyboard, a smile spreads across her face. "Ah, it looks like we actually have one left. It's on the top floor so you'll have a perfect view of the city, but it is a bit more expensive than our other rooms. Will that be okay?" she asks Chase, her eyes briefly darting to me, still partially hidden behind him. I grab a fistful of the back of Chase's shirt and nod my head okay when he looks back at me questioningly. The price doesn't matter, all we need right now is a place to stay.

Luckily, he seems to come to the same conclusion as me. "That will work. How much?" He asks as he reaches into his back pocket and pulls out his wallet.

She glances down at the computer screen and types on the keyboard a few more times before flashing Chase a bright smile. "Looks like your total will come to $571.93."

My eyes widen before I can stop myself. Chase's movements momentarily halt, his hand paused over his wallet, before he quickly recovers and fishes out the card. It's funny; there was a time not too long ago when I wouldn't have even blinked at that number, but after spending a lot of time in those cheap motels, it feels strange to spend this much for a night.

Jessica charges the card then hands it over to Chase along with our room key. "Alright, you're all set. You'll be in room 405. If you need anything else just let me know, my name's Jessica."

"Great. Thanks," Chase says tightly. I can tell he hates the idea of spending that much money on a room for one night. He starts to walk away when he turns back to Jessica suddenly. "Oh, could we also get two bottles of water please."

"Sure, I'll go get them." She walks over to a little alcove connected to the front desk that has a wall of snacks. I lean over the counter slightly to watch as she pulls out two waters from a little mini fridge. I straighten back up when she comes back toward us, and he takes the waters from her outstretched hands.

"Thank you," he tells her and then turns, heading toward the elevators on the other side of the room. I hurriedly follow behind him and he jabs his finger against the up arrow a little more forcefully than necessary. The elevator pings, the doors sliding open and we get in. He again hits the number four with force, the round button lighting up. The ride up is quiet, neither one of us saying anything, and the air feels thick. I stare at my reflection in the mirrored door and am still shocked by my looks. From my dirty brown hair under my baseball cap to my baggy clothes, I doubt anyone would recognize me now.

I see the digitized number four light up overhead just as the elevator stops and the doors open. I trail Chase as he walks down the hallway, making a left and then a right, before we finally come to a stop in front of our door. Room 405. As soon as we walk inside, I can see that the room is a lot like how it was downstairs. It has pops of dark green instead of gold throughout, but the ceiling is the same black as the lobby. It's dark and cozy and I kind of love it.

I set Emma's car seat on the ground and reach down to get her out. "I can do that," Chase says, unbuckling her.

"Okay," I whisper. I walk over to the window and pull back the curtains, but I can't see much. A few scattered lights glimmer in what I'm assuming is the downtown area, making everything seem sort of peaceful.

Chase comes up behind me with Emma in his arms, and we both stare out the window in comfortable silence. "I don't know if it's an almost six-hundred-dollar view, but it's not too bad."

I snort and turn around to look up at him. "Yeah, it's not bad at all."

He stares down at me with a smile, and I almost stop breathing. His blue eyes sparkle more than I remember, and I find myself leaning into him slightly. He opens his mouth, and I wait in suspense to see what he will say. Right then, Emma flails her arms, accidently whacking Chase in the face. I can't help but laugh at Chase's expression while muttering my apologies.

He shakes his head at Emma while bouncing her lightly in his arms. "Hey, I thought you were starting to like me."

I smile at the two of them. "She does like you," I whisper.

"You think so?" he offers me a half smile, making my cheeks turn pink. He stares at me a beat, and suddenly, his breathing starts getting faster. There's a charge in the air, like the room is slowly being sucked of its oxygen, before he breaks this weird connection by quickly turning his attention to Emma. I try to ignore the twinge of disappointment and turn to find Emma giving Chase a gummy smile.

"See, she's smiling at you."

"Don't babies smile at everything?" He asks with a laugh, repeating my earlier statement.

I playfully hit his arm. "You know what I mean."

"Uh-huh. You want to go to your momma while I get you a bottle?" He asks Emma, and hands her to me without waiting for my answer. He grabs the formula out of Emma's bag and takes one of the water bottles from the desk, pouring it into her bottle. I watch him as he carefully scoops out some of the formula and mixes it with the water in her bottle. I know, I *know*, he's just trying to be helpful, but tonight feels different. Maybe it's because of that charged moment we just shared, or the fact that this might be our last night together, but I'm suddenly feeling very out of my depth here and want to get back on familiar ground.

"I'll feed her," I blurt with more force than intended. He stares at me, his surprise evident on his face, and I find myself wanting to backtrack. "I just meant, um, that I could do that. You know, uh, if you didn't want to ..." I trail off, letting my words hang in the air between us.

His jaw flexes as he slowly sets the bottle back down on the desk in front of him. I'm rooted in my spot by the window, unable to move or breathe. He doesn't look at me as he answers. "No, you're right; it's your place. I'm going to go get our bags from the car."

Without waiting for my reply, he turns and walks to the door. I'm finally jolted out of my frozen state and want to call out after him; to tell him I didn't mean it. "Chase—" I start to say, but it's a weak attempt, the door already closing behind him with a resounding *click*.

I stand there, staring at the door, tears welling behind my eyes. I release the breath I had been holding and hang my head. I basically just told him to get lost while he was doing an incredibly nice thing for me. Why did I have to say that? After all that progress we made, I feel like I just completely smashed it to bits. I couldn't help it; seeing the way he took charge to care for Emma did something to my heart. But the truth is, after tomorrow, he'll leave us, and I'll need to figure things out on my own. Getting caught up in the idea of him always being here for us isn't something I need to be doing right now. A groan slips past my lips as I walk over and pick up the discarded bottle.

Chase comes back in with our bags just as Emma finishes her bottle, not saying a word to me. I don't ask what took him so long because I can probably guess it has something to do with me. He places our bags near the end of the bed and rummages through until he grabs some of his clothes.

"I'm going to take a shower," he states, looking at me to gauge my reaction. Even though he's hurt by my callous response earlier, I know he still wants to make sure I don't need anything.

"Okay," I tell him. With a nod, he walks over to the bathroom and shuts the door. I finish feeding Emma and burp her. I can hear the shower still running, so I set up her crib, change her diaper, and get her ready for bed. Once she's all tucked in, I grab my pajamas from my suitcase, figuring it'll still be a minute before Chase is out of the bathroom. I tug my jeans down and put on a pair of sleep shorts. I pull my shirt over my head but am met with some resistance, realizing it somehow got snagged on the clip of my bra.

"Oh, come on." I groan, my voice muffled by the fabric as I try to wrestle it free. I reach around stiffly and unclasp my bra, feeling the shirt start to give. Excitedly, I pull the shirt off the rest of the way. "Yes!" I cry out, right as the door to the bathroom opens and Chase walks out, enveloped in steam.

He stops in his tracks when he notices me, and we both freeze, staring at each other. I quickly jerk my shirt down in front of me, covering up my bra that is now hanging loosely off my shoulders. Chase continues to stand there, unblinking, as he stares at me. I can feel the heat crawling up my neck as a blush spreads across my face. I was so focused on getting my shirt off that I never heard the shower turn off. It's only then, when he's standing right in front of me, that I notice what he's wearing for the first time.

My mouth suddenly dries up from looking at him and I swallow a few times to get working again. His brown hair is still damp from the shower, with strands of it falling in front of his eyes and sticking to his brow. I slowly lower my gaze, watching as his muscles lightly flex beneath his T-shirt, sending ripples down his arms. Gray sweatpants cling to his waist and I bite back a groan at how good they look on him. He clears his throat, and my eyes snap back up to his, a small smirk playing at the corner of his lips. He knows he just caught me accidentally checking him out. My face feels overheated, and I look away, embarrassed.

"Sorry I took so long."

"Huh?" I look back at him, surprised by the huskiness in his voice. He points to the bathroom behind him and I shake my head, trying to clear it. "Right, uh, it's all good." I cringe as soon as the words leave my mouth, wishing the floor would swallow me up. Without waiting for him to reply, I drop my arms and start walking towards the bathroom, wanting to get out of here as fast as possible.

"Tatum," he growls, making me stop short. I tilt my head in confusion when I see him looking up at the ceiling. He lifts his arm and waves it around in my direction. "Your shirt."

My eyes practically bug out of my head when I look down and realize that in dropping my arms, I also dropped my shirt, baring my chest to him. Mortified, I let out a small squeak as I quickly cover myself and flee to the bathroom. I hear his light chuckle on the other side of the door as I slam it shut and lean back against it, closing my eyes. I push off the door and notice that I never brought the shirt I was planning to sleep in with me. I shrug and say *screw it*, slipping my bra down my arms and putting the shirt that gave me so much trouble back on. Turning on the tap, I splash some water on my face to cool my burning cheeks. I linger a little longer than usual, hoping that Chase may have fallen asleep already so we can avoid talking about what just happened.

I slowly open the door, inch by inch, trying not to make a sound, and peek out. The room is dark except for the faint glow of Emma's white noise machine. I tiptoe quietly over to the bed and discover that while my head was a basket case of emotions, I failed to notice there's only one bed. Again. In true Chase form, he's lying on top of the sheets with a thin blanket covering him, his chest slowly rising and falling. I exhale and climb into the bed, snuggling under the covers. I turn on my side to face his back, tucking my hands under my head and watch the steady rhythm of his breathing. A part of me is nervous being this close to him, while the other part kind of wishes he would get under the covers with me so I could feel his warm body heat surrounding me.

"Night, Tatum," Chase murmurs sleepily, his hand reaching back around him to find mine. He gives it a gentle squeeze, and my eyes go wide before a small smile pulls at my lips. It's a simple gesture, but one that reassures me we're okay and he's not upset for how I acted earlier.

"Goodnight, Chase," I tell him softly. Closing my eyes I drift off, a smile still on my face.

Emma wakes me up bright and early the following morning. The first thing I see when I wake up to the sound of her cries, is the blanket bunched at Chase's waist with his arm outstretched towards me. We're facing each other, and I take the opportunity to study him. From the way his brown hair flops over his forehead to his rough, calloused hands. He's sleeping so peacefully that even though I want to take all the time to memorize his every feature, I don't want to disturb him. I get out of bed as quietly as possible to avoid waking him up. I pick up Emma from her crib, her cries calming down now that she's in my arms. I take her to the bathroom, where I feed her so Chase can sleep some more. She's almost done with the bottle when I hear a shrill ringing from my phone.

I put her bottle down and race back into the room and grab the phone. Chase sits up suddenly. "What's going on?" he asks. He looks down at the ringing phone in my hands. "Is that Courtney?"

I nod wordlessly. He quickly jumps into action, throwing off the blanket, and rushing towards me. He grabs the phone out of my hands and answers it, putting it on speaker.

"Hello," he answers, his voice thick with tension.

"Chase?" Courtney's whisper comes across the line. My heart is beating wildly, waiting to hear our fate. Finally, I find my voice.

"Court," I say nervously.

"Tatum," she sighs in relief, "I got worried for a second."

"I was feeding Emma," I mumble distractedly. My heart picks up speed. "Why were you worried?"

"I just hadn't heard from you and then Chase answers ... my mind went to worst case scenario."

Chase rolls his eyes. "Of course you did."

I can tell she's about to argue with him, but I need to know why she called. "Court, what's going on?"

"Oh, right," she sighs, and I hear rustling in the background. "Sorry it's so early, but I wanted to call as soon as I could." She hesitates and I don't like it. She wouldn't call unless she had news about our situation. "I, um, well there was this event I went to last night. You know that Empowering Lives charity gala I usually avoid like the plague? Well, I went to it because I knew your mom would be there and I wanted to find out any information if I could ..." she pauses again, and I swallow roughly. "Tatum, I love my brother, but do you want him to hear this?"

I look up at Chase, the guy who took on this challenge and has been by my side— the guy who told me about his past and his mom. I nod my head even though she can't see it. "Yeah, just tell us, Court."

She sighs. "I just want to warn you first that this is not your fault. This is on them, okay? Not you." My hands start to feel clammy, and I sit down on the bed, rocking Emma in my arms.

"Okay," I whisper.

She takes a deep breath. "From what I was able to gather ... they're not looking for you," she murmurs sadly. The air leaves my lungs and if I wasn't already sitting, I would've fallen down. This is the news we were hoping for, right? Then why does it feel so wrong?

"What did she say exactly?" I ask, noticing that Chase is suspiciously quiet.

She hesitates a beat before saying, "That you got early admission into Columbia." I suck in a sharp breath. If Courtney hears, she doesn't acknowledge it, instead barreling on like she's ripping off a Band-Aid. "I overheard her telling some people that while you were 'modeling in France' last year—aka when you were pregnant with Emma—you graduated online early. Then, you spent your summer at an internship in the city and got accepted to Columbia. Now you're there, working *very hard* and *making us all proud*, according to her. And poor Adam is *absolutely heartbroken* that the two of you broke up so that you could pursue your career," she spits out. "Like I said, Tatum, this is on them, not you."

All I can do is stare at the phone in Chase's hand, my ears ringing like everything is underwater. I grip Emma to me tightly, unsure if I want to laugh, cry, or scream. I feel a brush of fingertips on my arm, and I look up to find Chase staring back at me, concern etching his features.

"They invented a whole other life for me," I whisper to no one in particular.

Chase shakes his head, but it's Courtney who answers. "No, they told a lie because they're too afraid of what people might think if they found out the truth. And trust me, the truth isn't that you had Emma. It's that they aren't good parents and would rather come up with an elaborate lie than for people to know that they aren't looking for you. All this does is reiterate that you're doing the right thing for *your* daughter."

Tears well in my eyes and I swipe at them angrily. I'm upset with myself for shedding tears over them and I'm furious at the realization that they genuinely don't care about me. Overall, I'm just plain angry at them. At the fact that their image means *everything* to them. More than making sure their daughter, and their granddaughter, are okay.

"Tatum," Courtney's soft voice comes over the speaker. I just shake my head, the words not forming. Chase squeezes my arm once before taking the phone off speaker and moving away from me. He talks to Courtney in hushed whispers that I can't hear. He glances back at me and sighs, walking back to where I'm sitting. He flips the phone back on speaker and holds it out to me. I don't take it, but I hear Courtney on the line.

"I'm really sorry, Tatum. I didn't want to tell you, but you deserve to know the truth. You know I'm always here for you."

"Forever and always," I choke.

"Forever and always," she replies with a smile in her voice. "I'll let you go because I know the two of you probably need to get on the road, but you are so much stronger than you realize. Remember that."

"I will. Thanks for calling, Court. It's really good to hear your voice."

She sniffles. "Yeah, yeah, I miss you too. Now, go take care of my goddaughter and don't forget to call once you're settled down. Oh! Look on the bright side, you're technically not on the run anymore." She laughs and without a goodbye, hangs up.

Chase and I sit in silence, the room suddenly too quiet. Emma babbles in my arms and I get up to grab her discarded bottle. Chase watches as I pace back and forth around the room while I feed Emma.

"You okay?" he asks cautiously.

I shrug and shake my head. "I honestly don't know."

He sits down on the foot of the bed and braces his forearms on his knees. "Courtney's right, you know. This is on them."

I nod. "I know that. I *know* they're not good parents. But it doesn't make it sting any less to know that they'd make up this entire new life for me rather than make sure I was okay. Hell, make sure I was even still alive. I could've been kidnapped for all they know, and they would never find me because they're not even looking!" I yell, startling Emma. I can tell she's about to cry so I shush her and gently bounce her in my arms. I shake my head in exasperation and sit beside Chase on the bed. "The fact is they just don't care. And I knew that they didn't, not really, but hearing it confirmed just," I sigh sadly, "hurts."

He nods. "I can't say I know what you're going through right now, but I do get it. Having a parent, or parents, who don't give a shit about you sucks." I blink up at him through teary eyes. "But like Courtney said, you're a lot stronger than you give yourself credit for. What you're doing for Emma," he shakes his head and looks at her in my arms, "it's incredible." He reaches out and brushes a finger across her cheek. She blinks up at him and wraps her little finger around his. He smiles down at her and it's the first time I've seen him look at her as adoringly as he is right now. My heart seems to skip a beat, and butterflies erupt in my belly. And just like that, the sadness from my past evaporates and is replaced by hope. Hope for the future—hope that my daughter never knows the feeling of not being loved.

Chase clears his throat, and our little intimate moment is over. "You ready to get on the road?"

I nod and we head out to the car. Once we're both buckled in, I turn to him. "Now where do we go?"

He looks over at me. "My mom used to talk about a small town she would visit that was only a few hours away from where she grew up. It was right on the beach and since she grew up in the mountains, she always loved going there. She said she was the happiest when she was at the beach. I was thinking maybe we could check out that place first? See if you like it enough to stay there?"

"I'd love that." I grab our faithful paper map. "Uh, do you remember the name of the town?" I ask, trying to read the small print on the map.

"Here, let me see it," he says, grabbing the map from my hands. I watch silently as his eyes scan it. "It looks like we can keep following this route before taking the split north of LA. I think it should take about seven and a half, eight hours, max," he says confidently.

"Wow. And then we'll be there," I say.

"Yup, we'll finally be there," he agrees.

The drive has become more relaxed now that we know we're not being followed. There's a carefree ease in the air as we drive over the state line. I look over and catch him smiling, a look of peace on his face as we pass the big California sign. A smile spreads across my own face as I watch him, determined to savor this moment. After everything he went through with his mom, I hope I can at least bring him some semblance of joy out of this, and if that means going to one of her favorite spots, then so be it. I can't imagine what must be going through his mind, being only a few hours away from the town she loved, fueling that connection that has faded ever since she passed away. I can see the eagerness to get there emanating from him. I close my eyes and take a deep breath, knowing that everything will change once we get there, but for once, I'm excited about what the future will hold.

I feel a wave of excitement when we pass the town limit sign and gaze out the windshield in awe of the charming little town. Small shops line both sides of the road, and a bright sign for an ice cream shop catches my attention on one of the corners. The town itself sits right by the ocean, a vibrant sunset floating over the horizon. We drive past a restaurant that looks more like a large shack, with a spacious outdoor seating area. The place is packed with people laughing and talking around the tables. It's situated right on the beach, offering impeccable ocean views, with sand spilling onto the wooden floorboards. I continue to stare at it as we pass by, completely enchanted with this town. No wonder his mom loved this place so much.

We drive a few more blocks until we stop at a small hotel right across the street from the beach. It's only a two-story building but looks a thousand times nicer than most of the motels we've stayed in before. Chase pulls in, parks the car in a spot right up front, and looks over at me.

"What do you say? One more night for old times' sake?" he asks, humor lacing his voice.

I laugh and shake my head. "Fine, but this had better be the last time. I don't know how much more I can take."

"Promise. After tomorrow, there'll be no more hotels or motels in your future."

"I'm holding you to that."

I get Emma out and start to walk towards the check-in area but stop short when I notice he's not following me. I turn and find him watching me. "What?" I ask, feeling self-conscious.

"Does this mean you want to stay here then?"

I look around before casting my gaze back to him. My eyes drift down to Emma, all snuggled in her car seat. I watch the orange hues of the sunset stream across her face and take a moment to bask in the peacefulness of it. I wasn't entirely sure if this was where I wanted to stay until this very moment. Something beautiful settles in my heart; I don't know whether it's the connection to Chase's mom or the ocean calling me, but I do know this feels right. It feels like home.

"Yeah, I think I do," I say, feeling more confidence with this decision than I have in a long time. I smile at Chase, enjoying this little moment and all that has led us here.

He laughs at me. "Come on. Let's go check in for the last time." We walk towards the entrance together as a sense of contentment washes over me. It feels like we're all finally in the place we're meant to be.

CHAPTER 10

The morning sunlight filters through the curtains that hang slightly ajar in our room. I look at the bed beside mine and find Chase still sleeping soundly. I don't blame him; I think this is the first night I've actually got some decent sleep. Even though we're still in a hotel, something about this place feels different. Maybe it's the atmosphere of this town, or perhaps it's because of the decision I made last night, to stay here. I feel a tranquility that I haven't felt in a while. I throw back the covers and get up, needing to use the bathroom. As I pass by Emma's crib, I lean over it to check on her, surprised she hasn't woken up yet. She's there, sleeping as peacefully as Chase, and I smile to myself at how cute they both are.

I walk over and turn off the white noise machine but stop short when I hear it still going. Confused, I squint down at it, thinking I must not have turned it off. I reach over to press the power button again, but notice that the light is already off. It takes me a minute, but when it finally dawns on me, I race over to the window and whisk back the curtains. The sun glistens off the water, and I can see the waves lapping at the shore. It's not the white noise machine I was hearing, but the actual sound of the ocean just across the way.

"What's going on?" I hear Chase mumble groggily from behind me. I turn around and see that the sunlight pouring in from the opening in the curtains is directly on his face, his hand raised to shield his eyes from it.

I wince. "Sorry about that." I drop the curtain, and the light fades from his face. He lowers his hand and looks at me expectantly. "I guess I forgot where we were for a second. I thought Emma's white noise machine was glitching or something until I realized it was the ocean I was hearing." I wave my hand in the direction of the curtains and pause as the sound of waves crashing against the shore slowly drifts into the room.

He stretches his arms high above his head. "That's a nice way to wake up. What time is it?"

"No idea," I reply, shaking my head as I glance at the clock on the nightstand. He follows my line of sight, and his eyes widen, when we see that it's just after nine.

"I think this is the latest we've slept in."

I nod in agreement. "I can't believe Emma's still sleeping too."

He looks over to her crib is, and a smile takes over his face. "I think she likes it here."

"I think you're right." I tell him, returning his smile.

We stare at Emma in silence before he breaks it by throwing the covers off and getting out of bed. I quickly avert my stare as a blush creeps up my neck. I'm so used to seeing him in his basketball shorts or sweatpants that I'm momentarily stunned when he stands up and is just wearing boxers and a shirt. He walks over to his discarded jeans that are slung over the chair in the room and starts pulling them up his legs.

"I'll run down to the front desk and see if there's a breakfast place around here. Do you want me to ask them if they have any idea about finding an apartment?"

I finally look back at him. "Yeah, that'd be great. Thanks."

He snatches up his wallet and keys before heading out the door. I go over and wake Emma up to get her fed. Chase is back by the time she finishes the last of her bottle.

"Apparently there's a pretty good bakery in town just up the road and," he pauses and holds up a little white piece of paper, "I got a card for a realtor here."

"That's great!" I beam. "I just fed Emma, but I still need to change her diaper and take a shower, then I'll be ready to go."

"I can change her while you shower," he says with a confidence he hasn't had before.

"Are you sure?" I ask.

He nods. "I should probably learn how to." I narrow my eyes at him suspiciously, not sure how I should take that. Before I can question him, though, he's grabbing a diaper from her bag. "Alright, how do I do this?"

I go through the motions of explaining how to take her diaper off, use a wet wipe, and make sure the new diaper is secured on her just right. "You want to make sure that it's tight enough to where nothing will leak out, but loose enough that it won't pinch her."

He nods along, intently listening to me as I speak. "Okay, I think I can handle that."

"Okay …" I say slowly. I grab my clothes and walk hesitantly towards the bathroom, quietly watching him change her diaper with an efficiency I didn't know he had. He talks to her softly while he does, whispering and smiling down at her. I gaze at the two of them as he says something and tickles her belly, getting a giggle out of her. I quickly turn before he discovers me standing there watching him and walk into the bathroom.

Once the door is shut behind me, I brace my hands against the counter and stare at my reflection in the mirror. I try to imagine what he must think when he looks at me. Makeup hasn't touched my face in weeks, and dark circles are forming under my eyes. My brown hair has faded slightly, making it look duller than it did before. Overall, I feel like I barely recognize myself anymore.

I take a deep breath and step into the shower, taking my time washing my hair. I take these few minutes to remind myself that it's okay to change. Even if I don't necessarily recognize myself, that doesn't mean it's a bad thing. I know I've changed within; it's just now reflected back at me when I look in the mirror Once I get out of the shower, I pull on my favorite hoodie, wanting all the comfort it provides for today.

When I walk out of the bathroom, I find Chase lightly bouncing Emma in his arms in front of the window, looking out at the ocean and speaking to her in hushed tones. I lean against the doorframe and take a few seconds to watch them, wanting to hold onto this image of them forever. My heart constricts at how he's treated her this whole time we've been together. I can only hope that one day we'll be lucky enough to find someone to treat us the way he has. Hating that I have to ruin this moment between them, I put my stuff down on my suitcase loudly.

"Are you ready to go?"

He looks back at me, oblivious to me watching them, and nods. "Yup."

We load up the car with the rest of our things and make our way back into town. The town is a strip of shops along the road, with a single traffic light in the middle. There's a bookstore, a coffee shop, a boutique, and two restaurants scattered amongst other stores that appear to be offices. It's not a large town, but it's cute and quaint, and I love it already. Even though there aren't too many people wandering around, it still seems pretty busy for ten o'clock on a weekday. Chase finds an open parking spot along the street and parks the car. We get out, and I quickly unhook Emma's car seat before meeting Chase on the sidewalk. I follow him as we pass by a few shops until we come to a stop in front of a little bakery on the corner. A big pink sign hangs over the door, spelling out *Sweet Treats*.

"This is it," Chase says, nodding up to the sign before opening the door and ushering us inside. The sweet smell of baked goods fills my nostrils as soon as I walk in. I look around at the wooden tables dispersed around the shop and notice that we're the only customers here. In front of us is a glass display case filled to the brim with an assortment of treats ranging from bagels to doughnuts to muffins. My mouth waters at the sight of them and my stomach chooses that moment to rumble loudly. Luckily, before I can feel embarrassed about that or before Chase can say anything, a woman comes out of the back carrying a large tray of doughnuts.

She startles when she sees us, but quickly plasters on a bright, friendly smile. She sets down the tray on the back counter and turns to greet us. "Hi there! Sorry, I didn't hear you come in. Can I get you anything?"

My eyes dart from the board behind her, trying to read over the list of everything they offer, to the glass case where I can see all the delicious baked goods. "Um, I'm not sure. They all look so good," I say.

"Well, thank you. My husband and I make them fresh every day," she says, smiling proudly at me. "But our most popular ones are the chocolate chip and blueberry muffins, the lemon custard doughnut, and my personal favorite, the cinnamon sugar swirl doughnut."

I bite my lip, debating the choices. "I think I'll go with the cinnamon sugar swirl doughnut, then." I smile at her. If it's her favorite, then I know it'll be good.

"Excellent choice," she says, giving me a wink and then looking at Chase expectantly.

"I'll do the chocolate chip muffin. And two coffees, please."

"Sure," she nods and grabs two plates from under the counter. "Cream or sugar?"

"Both," Chase tells her.

She nods and walks over to the coffee machine behind her.

Picking up two blue mugs, she fills them each with coffee, leaving a little room at the top. After adding the cream and sugar, she uses a tall spoon to mix everything together. Carefully gripping the mug by their handles, she turns slowly so as not to spill and sets them on the counter in front of us. Then she reaches into the glass display case with all the treats and grabs the chocolate chip muffin first, before grabbing my doughnut. Once she places them on the plates in front of us, she heads to the register.

"Alright, that'll be $14.45," she says. Chase reaches into his back pocket and gets his wallet out. She watches us as he does so. "So, are you two new around here?"

"That obvious?" I chuckle nervously.

"Nah," she says, shaking her head. Chase hands her a twenty-dollar bill and she opens the register drawer, counting out his change. "It's just we don't get a lot of new faces around here."

I glance over at Chase, unsure how to respond, and thankfully he takes my cue without missing a beat. "Yeah, we just got into town last night. We're actually going to stop over at Lewis Realty after we eat." He tells her, reciting the name on the card he got from the hotel.

Her entire face lights up at the mention of that, smiling so wide I worry that her cheeks may start hurting. "Oh! Well, in that case, here's a little treat you can give to Mary." She hands Chase his change, and walks over to the glass display case, pulling out what looks like a blueberry muffin. She places it into one of the brown paper to-go bags lying on the counter. With her back turned slightly away from us, she doesn't notice when Chase drops all the change she gave him into the little tip jar beside the register; but I do. I say nothing as she turns back to us and hands the bag to Chase. He takes it from her outstretched hand with a small, tight smile. "It's her favorite. Just tell her it's from Sarah if you don't mind." She pauses and then adds, "on the house of course."

"Will do."

I pick up my coffee in one hand, Emma's car seat in the other, and walk over to a small table nestled in the front corner window of the shop. It has a great view of the street, and I want to watch all the people walk by. I set the car seat down next to me, intending to go back to get my doughnut, when Chase walks up with his hands full. He's got both plates balanced skillfully on his hand and forearm, and his coffee mug in the other.

"I was going to go back and get that," I mumble as he carefully sets his coffee mug down first and then places the plates on the table, sliding mine over in front of me.

He sits down in his chair and gets comfortable. "I thought I'd save you the trip," he says, unwrapping the parchment paper around the bottom of the muffin.

I settle down in my own seat and run my hand along the edge of my plate, debating what I want to say next. Without looking at him I say, "Why didn't you use the Visa card?"

When I'm met with silence, I risk a glance at him, only to find him staring down at his plate. If I'm not mistaken, it looks like there's a slight blush coloring his cheeks.

I watch as he takes a bite of his muffin without answering me. He chews and swallows, wiping some crumbs from the corner of his mouth. Finally, he shrugs and says, "I wanted it to be my treat. You know, as your first meal in your new home."

I suck in a breath, surprised by his gesture. "Thank you," I say quietly, unsure how to take that. Instead, I pick up my doughnut and bite into it. As soon as I do, flavors of cinnamon burst in my mouth, and I can't help but moan at how good it is. The dough is fluffy yet crispy on the outside, and every bite tastes amazing. "This is the best thing I've ever tasted," I say out loud, Chase chuckling lightly at me.

We finish eating in silence, and as I polish off the rest of my coffee, I glance up and find him watching me with a thoughtful expression on his face.

"Everything okay?" I ask.

"Yeah," he nods and leans forward, folding his arms and resting his elbows on the table. "It's just weird, you know? Being in this place."

"Yeah, I can only imagine," I say as I look out the window. He clears his throat, and I turn my attention back to him.

"I was thinking, maybe I could stay with you and Emma for the time being," he looks at me hesitantly, "instead of trying to find separate places? It might be easier if we can stay together."

I blink up at him as my heart skips a beat. I don't want to read too much into it, but this is what I hoped for. Even though I promised myself I could do this on my own, I like having him with me. I realize I've been quiet for too long because he starts to shift uncomfortably in his seat.

"If you're not okay with it, I understand. I can help you find a place to stay and get you settled in and then I'll look at different places I could go—"

"No!" I shout, startling us both, and he looks at me with wide eyes. "I mean, no, please stay. I guess I zoned out there for a second. I didn't mean for you to think that I—" I take a deep breath and say softer this time, "what I mean is I'd love it if you stayed with us."

His mouth twitches as he fights a smile. "Well okay then."

I take a deep breath and nod, smiling at him. "Okay then."

We get up and wave our goodbyes to Sarah as we head out the door. A cool breeze hits my face when I step outside, and I take a deep breath of the salty air. We cross the street and walk along the sidewalk. Chase stops suddenly and points to something.

"Look," he says. I turn my gaze to a flyer on one of the shop windows we're in front of. I look closely and realize it's a flyer for a garage hiring in town called *Miller's Motors*. I grab the flyer from off the window. "What are you doing?" Chase asks.

"Keeping it," I tell him. "Maybe we can check it out later. I mean, this does kind of seem like fate."

He chuckles and shakes his head. "You would think it's fate. Come on, let's tackle one thing at a time."

We keep walking until we spot the realtor's office. It's not hard to find, with its big red letters spelling *Lewis Realty* painted on the front window. Chase opens the door and motions for us to go inside ahead of him. The first thing I notice is the back wall, which is entirely covered in a sea life mural. The top half is a bluish-green wave, mid-spiral, with whitecaps at the very tip of it. A painted sun sits in the corner, set against a bright blue background for the sky. The bottom half holds all my attention, though; depicting an underwater scene of marine life. The sandy ocean floor is across the bottom of the wall, where crabs dart along it and seaweed floats up from it. There's a collection of various fish swimming about, and even a pod of dolphins. My favorite part is the brown treasure chest in the center, filled to the brim with gold coins and beautiful jewelry.

"Ah, yes. The mural."

A voice pulls me from the artwork. Chase and I turn our heads to see an older woman coming out of a room off to the side, holding a steaming cup of coffee. She looks like she could be in her late fifties or early sixties at most, with gray roots blending into her auburn-colored hair, and wrinkle lines around her eyes and mouth.

The woman looks at us. "This used to be a daycare for kids, and I bought it from them when they moved to the other side of town. I've been telling my husband he needs to paint over it, but it's been seven years now, and look what's still here." She waves her hand in front of her face, and I sense that this is a conversation she's had many times before. "Anyhoo, you don't need to listen to my story. What brings you two in today?" Her question trails off as her gaze darts between the two of us and then down to Emma. I can see her brows furrowing as a crease forms on her forehead, and I get the feeling she's trying to calculate how old we are and why we have a baby with us.

"We just got into town last night," Chase says politely. He lifts the to-go bag with the muffin in her direction. "Sarah asked us to give this to you." There's no use in hiding that fact since we already told Sarah back at the bakery; news probably travels fast in a place like this.

Her face softens at the mention of Sarah as she takes the bag from Chase's hand. "Oh, that girl knows the way to my heart," she says, glancing into the bag and spotting the blueberry muffin. She looks back up at us and shakes her head, cheeks going pink. "Sorry, I'm Mary Lou, but you can call me Mary. Everyone does."

I guess we got the stamp of approval with the muffin, I think.

Chase reaches out to shake her hand. "Nice to meet you, Mary. I'm Chase and this is Tatum." I wave to her with my free hand, the other still holding Emma's car seat.

"Tatum," she says, as if testing it out. "What a pretty name."

I blush at the compliment. "Thank you."

I peek at Chase, and he gives me a soft smile before turning his attention back to Mary. "We're moving here and need help finding a place to live."

"Of course! Let me see what we have. Please, come sit down," she replies, motioning us forward to the desk against the left wall. There's only one other desk in here, but it doesn't have much on it, giving no indication if it's being used or not. Chase and I take a seat in the two chairs in front of the desk, and I put Emma down in between us. She's been quiet this whole time and I glance down to see that she's focused on one of the toys I attached to the handle of the car seat. Hopefully she stays entertained until we're done here.

Mary pushes a few papers aside on her desk, then folds her hands and looks up at us. "Now, are you looking to rent or buy something?"

"We'd like to rent an apartment," Chase says, glancing at me and adding, "at least for the time being."

She purses her lips slightly and nods. "Unfortunately, we don't have any apartments here. They tried to build some here a few years ago, but everyone on the city council vetoed those plans, leaving us with limited options. The nearest apartment complex is about thirty minutes north of here, up in Flat Sands Beach. I suggest looking there if you're set on living in an apartment. But, if you're okay with a rental house, I can look and see what we have available here." She shakes the mouse to wake up the older computer on her desk and clicks away on the keyboard. After a few minutes of watching her eyes dart back and forth across the computer screen, she sighs and looks at us with a downcast expression. "I'm sorry, but I'm not seeing anything available. As you can see, we're a small community, and we don't have many places to choose from in the first place."

My heart sinks the more I listen to her talk. I glance at Chase and see the frustration I feel reflected on his face. It's gone in a flash, but I know it was there. "Is there really nothing available?" I ask before I fully grasp what I'm saying. I can hear the pleading in my voice, but I'm powerless to stop it.

She raises an eyebrow in surprise and tilts her head. Her eyes flick to Chase before falling back on me. "May I ask how old you two kids are?"

"Almost twenty," Chase answers.

"I'll be eighteen in a few months," I say at the same time.

"I see." She nods thoughtfully, still watching us with a knowing look. "And the baby?"

"She's a little over five months old." I don't elaborate any more than that; just let it hang there in the air between us.

She sighs and leans back in her chair. "I have to ask—are you kids in some sort of trouble?" she asks in a serious tone.

I bite my lip and hesitate. I have no idea how this conversation will go. It seems like she asked out of concern, but it's hard to trust someone, especially someone we just met. I'm trying to think of a way to tell her that we desperately want to stay here without giving away the reason why, when Chase straightens up and leans forward slightly, bracing his forearms on the sides of his chair.

"Look, Mary, we're not in any trouble. We had kind of a rough situation back home and we wanted to have a fresh start somewhere new. Having a baby wasn't ideal for the people we were close to, so we're doing what we think is right to protect Emma. My mom loved this place, she used to tell me stories about it and one day hoped to get back here. She passed away recently, and I thought that it would be the perfect place for us to settle down in. We may be young, but I can promise you we're okay. We can provide a few months' rent up front if that would help."

Mary and I both stare at Chase with wide eyes. Mary recovers more quickly than I do, schooling her features and taking her time to really look at Chase. I wait with bated breath to see what she will do next. A glint of resolve appears in her eyes as she seems to come to some conclusion. She nods and slowly smiles at us.

"I'll tell you what—there's a place up the road that I know of. It's private, off the market, and available for rent by the owner only. I may be able to pull a few strings to get you in, if you're interested?"

"Yes, absolutely," I immediately agree. She chuckles at my enthusiasm, and Chase cracks a smirk my way.

"Well, I don't have any other appointments today. Why don't I lock up here, and you two can follow me over to the rental?"

CHAPTER 11

We pull up in the driveway of an older two-story ranch-style house. The green paint has faded from years of being in the sun, giving it more of a soft sage color now. The front door, though, is a bright turquoise blue that stands out and grabs your attention. There's a wrap-around front porch with two rocking chairs on the right and a swinging bench hanging from the ceiling of the roof on the left. To the right side of the house I can notice what looks like a small vegetable garden, the tomatoes visible in the wooden box.

We get out of the car and Chase gets Emma out of the back seat. We must be close to the ocean because I can hear the waves as soon as I open my door. Chase comes to stand next to me, Emma's car seat in hand while she sleeps soundly in it. We walk over to where Mary is waiting at the base of the stairs leading up to the house.

"It's right this way," she tells us.

Instead of leading us up the stairs, though, she continues to the right of the house, past the vegetable garden, and steps onto a stone pathway that winds around the side of the house. A small, one-story cottage stands just a few yards away from the main house. It's painted a bright yellow and has the same turquoise color door as the main house. Colorful flowers line the front of the cottage, and as I look over to my left, I see that I was right in my earlier assumption, because the ocean comes into view. We're slightly higher up, but I can see stairs at the far end of the grassy backyard leading down to the beach.

I turn my attention back to the cottage in front of me, our shoes reverberating on the stone walkway, when I feel a hand brush against the small of my back. I look up to see Chase staring ahead, his gaze scanning our surroundings, all while his hand is curved protectively around me. A warmth spreads through me at his gesture, and find myself relaxing into his touch, letting him guide me forward. As we get closer to the cottage, a blast of salty air hits me, and I take a deep breath of it.

"This is it," Mary tells us as she pulls a key from her pocket and unlocks the door. She gestures for us to go ahead of her once the door is open. "After you."

We walk into the sunny living room, the curtains drawn back to reveal the simple setup. Against the wall to the left is a small couch with two floral-printed chairs on either side of it and a wooden coffee table in the middle. They face the TV mounted on the wall to the right. Just past the living room is the kitchen with a round table in the middle and four seats surrounding it, with a vase of flowers on top.

"You have your living room here, as you can see, and a fully furnished kitchen," Mary says as she slides past us to walk further into the house. "There are two bedrooms down this hallway and a bathroom." I glance down the hallway directly in front of us, past the kitchen table, and see three doors. Two of them are opposite each other on either side of the hall, while the third is at the end between the two.

I walk down the hallway first and open the door to my left. Inside is a queen bed with royal blue bedding, a closet to the left, a dresser with a mirror over it, and a nightstand on either side of the bed. It's cute and minimal, with the walls painted a light shade of peach. I feel Chase come up behind me to view the room, so I go around him to look at the other room across the hall. This room about the same size as the first one, but it has a double bed instead. The walls are beautifully decorated in a collage of yellows, oranges, and pinks, giving it a sunset glow feel. There's a closet to the right and a dresser, but only one nightstand since the bed is pushed up against the back wall. This must mean that the last door is the bathroom. Just I start to move to check it out, I feel Chase slide up behind to me.

He bends down to whisper in my ear as he eyes the room in front of us. "What do you think?"

I turn and smile up at him, bringing our faces only an inch apart. "I love it," I whisper back.

"I thought so." His smile reaches his eyes, causing the corners of it to crinkle a little bit. We're close, our noses almost touching, and I hold my breath, feeling the racing of my heart as it picks up speed. I swallow hard and stare up into his clear blue eyes. I open my mouth to say something, anything, but nothing comes out. "You and Emma should take this room," he says, his breath fanning across my lips before he pulls back and turns, walking back down the hallway to where Mary is waiting.

I stand there shell-shocked, blinking at his retreating figure. It takes me a few seconds to regain my composure, and I feel the heat rushing to my cheeks when I do. I push off the doorframe that I hadn't realized I leaned against and walk back into the kitchen. I spot Chase leaning up against the granite countertop, Emma's car seat still gripped in his hand, talking to Mary. When they notice me, Mary smiles wide while Chase smirks.

"Well, what do you think of the place?" she asks me, eagerly awaiting my answer.

I glance at Chase briefly; his smirk is gone, and he nods ever so slightly. I tell her the truth. "I think this place is amazing."

She clasps her hands together. "Oh good. I was hoping you would say that."

"How much is it?" Chase asks her.

"It'll be six-fifty a month. You're also responsible for the utilities, of course," Mary replies.

Chase nods, then hesitates. "I do have a question, though." I tilt my head, confused about where he's heading with this, but Mary stands there patiently, waiting for him to continue. "Who lives in that house up there?" He gestures his head to the house we passed by earlier.

I'm ashamed to admit that I had already forgotten all about it. I was so caught up in this charming little cottage I didn't even think to ask about who we would be sharing a property with.

Mary smiles kindly in response. "I was wondering when you were going to ask that. That's my house." My eyebrows almost lift to my hairline, while Chase's eyes widen a fraction. Mary continues, though, ignoring our looks of surprise. "My husband and I live there. We don't normally rent this house out—we had it built as a guesthouse long ago—but when I saw the three of you, I thought it would be perfect."

We continue to stare at her until I blurt, "You live up there?" As soon as the words leave my mouth, I wince. An embarrassing blush rises to my cheeks because, of course, she lives there. That's what she just said.

Mary chuckles lightly. "I do."

"So, this technically isn't available then, is it?" Chase asks, a slight edge to his voice. My shoulders slump at hearing that.

"Technically, no. But as I said, there's not much else available around here, and since this is just sitting here, it may as well be put to good use."

"Well, thank you for offering to us. We really appreciate it—"

"We'll take it," I announce, interrupting Chase before he can say something about how we couldn't possibly stay here because it wouldn't be right, or something along those lines, because it seems like something he would do. Instead of being upset that I bulldozed over whatever he was going to say, Chase just laughs.

"Which is what I was about to say. We'd love to rent this house, thank you for offering it to us." He shoots me a pointed look, a smirk tugging at his lips, and I blush under his gaze.

Mary laughs and claps her hands, a big smile overtaking her face. "Excellent!" She ushers us back outside and turns to lock the door. "We can go back to my office and get everything straightened out where I'll give you a copy of the key and let you get settled in."

We both pause, causing Mary to stop and give us a questioning stare. "What do you need us to do?" Chase asks hesitantly and my heart rate increases.

Mary tilts her head as she studies us. "It's not much. I'll need to get both your driver's licenses to have on file and then have you two sign a few documents stating that you both agree to the terms and conditions of living here and that you'll pay the rent on time."

I know she's not asking for much, and based on her confused look, probably wondering why this is an issue. But the more I think about the potential consequences of having my name on any official document, the more my heart sinks. I see Chase's shoulders deflate, and I know he's coming to the same conclusion I have.

"I'm really sorry, Mary, but we can't do that. I promise you we have the money, but Tatum's name can't be on anything."

Even having his name on anything is risky, but I keep my mouth shut. Although the threat of my parents finding us isn't hanging over our heads right now, that doesn't mean it won't change in the future. I focus my attention on one of the stones along the pathway in front of me, not wanting to see the judgment on Mary's face. I'm sure she's coming to the realization that we're a bigger problem than she expected, and it won't be long now before she tells us we can't stay here anymore. I sense movement in my peripheral vision and glance up to see her tucking her hands in the back pocket of her jeans. She's watching me with a melancholy look of understanding that catches me off guard. Then she shifts her attention to Chase.

"Alright then. I need to get back to the office, but why don't you kids come over for dinner tonight and we can discuss a payment plan. If you still really want to stay here, I'll need three months' rent up front and for you to tell me what you kids are running from." She holds up her hand as Chase and I both open our mouths to object. "I know you said you left to keep the baby, but there's a reason you can't have your name on anything. I'll do what I can to help you out, but I can't do that if I don't know why. So, do we have a deal?"

Chase and I glance at each other. As much as we don't want to do that, she has a point. This is our only option to stay here and unless we want to find somewhere else to live, we don't really have a choice. Whatever he sees in my eyes relaxes him. He squares his shoulders and nods at Mary.

"Deal."

CHAPTER 12

We meet back at Mary's house for dinner later that evening. As we step onto her front porch, she opens the door and greets us with a kind smile. She guides us through her house, past the living room, and into the sprawling kitchen, where an aroma of spices hits my nose. A large bay window above the sink offers a perfect view of the ocean below.

"Have a seat." Mary motions to the walnut-stained table in the corner, and Chase and I sit down. I take Emma out of her car seat and hold her in my arms, while she babbles and playfully grabs a loose strand of my hair. I pull it out of her grip because she's surprisingly strong and glance up to notice Mary smiling fondly at us. Just then, an older man walks in and stops short when he sees us sitting at the table.

"Well, hi there," he says to us, walking over to kiss his wife on the forehead.

"We have some guests," she tells him, gesturing to us. "This is Chase, Tatum, and Emma." She places her hand on his chest in a loving gesture. "And this is my husband, Conrad."

"Nice to meet you, sir," Chase says, standing and extending his hand to shake Conrad's.

"You as well," he says as he grips Chase's hand.

"They'll be staying in our guest house," Mary explains.

Conrad grins. "Will they now?"

"Of course," she responds confidently. "Come sit, we have things to discuss." Mary sits in the chair opposite of me, leaving Conrad sitting across from Chase. As soon as Conrad sits down, Mary doesn't miss a beat to grill us. "Now, will you tell us why you can't use your ID?"

Chase speaks up before I can. "We can use my ID. It's Tatum's name that doesn't need to be on anything."

Mary gives him a look. "I heard you the first time. What I want to know is, will there be any trouble coming to my doorstep?"

I shake my head vehemently. "No, definitely not." I take a deep breath and decide to tell her everything. "As Chase mentioned earlier, my parents weren't happy that I had Emma. Then, about three weeks ago, my mother handed me adoption papers for me to sign over my rights as Emma's mom to her father's family." I pause when both Mary and Conrad glare at Chase distrustfully.

He shakes his head. "I'm not the father," he says, a hint of sadness in his voice that I don't have time to decipher. Their shoulders relax and they turn their attention back to me.

Continuing, I say, "Obviously I couldn't let that happen, so my best friend came up with this plan to help me run away with the help of Chase, her brother."

"Half-brother," he corrects.

I roll my eyes. "Half-brother. Anyway, we went on the run because I refused to give up my rights to her. It wasn't until yesterday morning that we found out my parents had created an elaborate story about me getting into Columbia early. Now, I guess, they're just not looking for me. We decided to come here because, as Chase told you, his mom used to come here to visit when she was younger."

Mary sucks in a deep breath but allows us to continue without any judgement on her face.

"Tatum was able to get her trust fund transferred to her before we left, which is why I said we can afford it. I also saw the flyer about the garage in town needing a mechanic earlier and was planning to apply there so I can have an income as well." Chase explains, sitting up straighter in his chair.

Conrad nods. "That's a smart idea."

"I still can't have my name on anything, though, in case my parents ever try to find me in the future," I add.

"Oh, you poor thing," Mary says as she gets up from her seat and hugs me, enveloping Emma and me in her arms. "I'm sorry you had to go through that, but you're so very brave for making a decision like that." I'm a little surprised that a grown adult would call me brave for what I did instead of scolding me for how dangerous it could have been or for leaving my family behind to protect my daughter. She shakes her head and lets go of us. "I don't understand what kind of parent wouldn't search for their child or grandchild."

"Shitty ones," Chase butts in.

That gets a chuckle out of Conrad. "You may be right about that," he agrees, and Mary gives him a stern look. "I'd say you kids have been through enough. We'll do what we can to help you out."

"Letting us stay here is more than enough," Chase says. He reaches into his pocket and pulls out an envelope. "We, uh, stopped at an ATM in town earlier and got the three months' rent." He slides the envelope of cash across the table.

"It's a small town," Mary says as she sits back down, "as I'm sure you're aware. You'll need a little more help than just a place to live. I'll take you to get a new ID tomorrow. A friend of mine works there and we shouldn't have any problems getting one with a new last name." I raise my eyebrows in disbelief, because I'm pretty sure that's not entirely legal, but Mary doesn't bat an eye as she turns her attention to Chase. "As for you—I know Miller down at the garage. Old grump has been looking for some extra help for a while now and I'm sure he'd be thrilled to have someone interested. You've worked at a garage before, I assume?"

Chase nods. "Yes ma'am. When I lived in Texas with my mom. My goal is to open my own garage one day."

She beams at him. "Well, that's wonderful. We'll go see him after we get Tatum her new ID."

Chase and I share a look. Everything seems to be happening very fast, but we also appreciate all the help they're offering. Chase smiles warmly at Mary. "Thank you, that would be great."

She waves him off. "It's no problem. Now, I promised the two of you some dinner. Are you hungry?"

My stomach chooses that moment to growl, and I blush bright red. "Starving. But please say it's not hamburgers. I don't think I could eat anymore fast food," I plead.

Mary laughs. "Just some pasta and my famous garlic bread. Do you need anything for Emma, dear?"

I shake my head no. "I already fed her a bottle before we came here."

"Perfect," she replies, clapping her hands together.

We eat our dinner with casual conversations. Mary and Conrad share stories about the town, explaining who some people are and what there is to do here. They tell us how they met in high school and got married after college. They don't delve into much detail about their life after they got married, and I don't pry. Though there's a sadness that lingers around them when talking about it, they quickly change the subject and ask us questions about our life before we left. Chase mentions his mom briefly and talks about growing up in Texas. I try not to huff at the fact that he opened up so easily over a plate of pasta when it took him two weeks to talk about it with me, but I understand. Mary and Conrad have a comforting way about them; it feels like being wrapped in a warm blanket. The more we talk, the more grateful I am that we stumbled across them.

Once dinner is over, Mary hands us the keys to the cottage. "Since you haven't settled in yet, I'll have breakfast ready at 10 tomorrow if you'd like to stop by."

Chase pockets the keys while I hold a sleepy Emma in my arms. "That would be wonderful, thank you. Usually, we've had gas station snacks or coffee for our breakfast," I grumble.

Conrad laughs. "Well, not anymore, kiddo." I look at him with a raised brow, wondering where that came from all of a sudden. He shrugs. "Thought it fit."

I smile warmly at him. "I like it."

After a hug goodbye, we leave and make the short trek to our new home. It's a little unbelievable how this has all come together, but what I'm most thankful for is not having to sleep in motels anymore.

Looking down at the shiny plastic card now, it feels surreal that I got here. That the girl in the picture, with the long brown hair and new last name, is me. Yesterday, after breakfast at their house, Mary took Chase and me to the DMV, just like she promised. Chase sat patiently with us, holding Emma, while Mary helped me fill out the paperwork. She truly does have power in this town because her friend didn't bat an eye when I got a new driver's license with a different last name on it. Afterward, we stopped by the garage where we met Miller—who really did seem like an old grump. However, Chase looked to be on cloud nine as Miller told him to come by and start working tomorrow. Then, we ended the day by having dinner at Mary's house again since we didn't have time to do any shopping.

I tuck the ID into the clear pouch of my wallet and toss it into my purse. After checking my outfit in the mirror one last time, I scoop up Emma from her crib. With her in my arms, I grab my purse and leave the room. I make sure to double-check I have everything I need for my interview this afternoon.

In addition to everything else Mary and Conrad have done for us, they also got me a job interview. I know I don't technically need the job, but it gives me something to do with my time before I can get my GED. I pick up Emma's bag from beside the couch—it has her toys, diapers, a burp cloth, and extra bottles—and leave the house. I make the short trek up the stone walkway to Mary's house and give a light knock on the door before entering.

"Mary, we're here," I call out as I walk in. I go into the kitchen and set Emma down in her bouncy seat, which now has a permanent spot beside the table. Remarkably, it was Conrad who bought it for her. When I asked him about it, he said, *she should be happy and comfortable over here any time she wants*. I grab the formula and bottle from her bag and set it on the table, intending to feed her before I leave.

"I can do that. You're going to be late for your interview," Mary says as she breezes in with a smile on her face.

"I still have, like, twenty minutes," I say, but I know she isn't really listening. She waves me aside and grabs the bottle from my hands, going over to coo at Emma. Emma babbles and smiles back at her, excited to see Mary's face. I roll my eyes, but a smile takes over my face as I watch the two of them. A pang of longing hits me, and I wish, just for a second, that my mother could have been like this. That she could've been someone who was happy to see Emma and would coo over her grandchild, taking care of her when I couldn't be there. I push that feeling aside, knowing it will never be like that, and lean against the counter.

"Are you sure you don't mind babysitting? With Chase starting his new job and me going for this interview, I haven't had time to get Emma into daycare."

She waves me off like I knew she would. "Nonsense. You know I'm happy to do it. You should get going before you're late." She leaves the kitchen and yells out, "Conrad, she's here. Time to go." I snicker as she comes back into the kitchen shaking her head. "I swear, that man."

"I'm old, not deaf," Conrad grumbles as he strolls into the kitchen, "you don't need to yell."

Mary huffs. "I yell because you somehow never seem to hear me when I need you to."

He taps his ear, smiling at her. "It's called selective hearing."

She rolls her eyes at him good-naturedly and I chuckle at them as they banter back and forth. I don't think I've ever heard my parents crack a joke in their life, let alone with each other.

"You ready to go, kiddo?" Conrad asks.

"Yup. All set."

"Good luck!" Mary calls out as we're walking out the door. I turn and find her in the kitchen, feeding Emma her bottle and smiling fondly at me.

It warms my heart, and I return her smile with one of my own. "Thank you."

We drive down to Flamingo's—the restaurant right on the beach that we passed by on our first night in town—with the radio on and the windows down. I hold my hair back in one hand so that it doesn't get too wind-blown, enjoying the salty breeze that rushes past me. Conrad turns on his blinker and pulls into the parking lot, stopping right in front of the entrance. The bright neon pink *Flamingo's* sign glows overhead, and although it's not as flashy during the day as it is at night, it's still overwhelming. There aren't too many cars here, but I suddenly feel nervous. Even though Mary helped me get this interview, it's up to me to get the job. I've never had a job before, and it's the uncertainty of not knowing what to expect that makes me tense.

Conrad must sense my hesitation about getting out of the car.

"You've got this kiddo," he says, patting my arm and giving me an encouraging nod.

I take a deep breath and open the car door. *I can do this.* As I step out, I tell myself there's nothing to worry about; it's just an interview at a local beach restaurant. I can't help but snort at the thought that my parents would probably have a heart attack if they could see me now.

"Thanks Conrad," I tell him through the open window. I straighten, rolling back my shoulders, and head for the door.

I walk into the restaurant and am immediately greeted by the smell of fried seafood. Pictures of fishermen on their boats, proudly holding different types and sizes of fish, adorn the wooden slat walls. Wooden tables are clustered throughout the open dining area, and just beyond that, garage-style windows are lifted and secured to the ceiling, leaving an unobstructed flow between the dining room and the outdoor patio deck. The deck, situated right on the beach, has sand spilling over onto the wooden floors. As I walk farther into the restaurant, I'm able to really take it in.

"Welcome to Flamingo's," a voice drawls from my left. "Are you dining in or picking up?" I turn and see a girl about my age, maybe a little older, lounging behind a black hostess stand looking bored.

"I'm, uh, actually here to see Mark?" I pause making sure I have the name right. "I have an interview with him."

Her mood instantly changes at that. She perks up and her eyes widen as she smiles. "Oh, thank gawd," she says, drawing out the *w* and making it more pronounced. She pops the gum that's in her mouth and rounds the hostess stand, coming to a stop in front of me. "I seriously thought he was going to try and make me come back for weekends if we couldn't find anyone. Like, I know I signed up for classes late and stuff, but I told Uncle Mark my priority was going to be school this year, not wasting all my time at his restaurant."

I glance around and confirm that we're the only ones here. "Right ..." I drag out, not sure what to say to her.

She just nods her head like she agrees with me. "His office is this way. Come on, I'll show ya."

She turns and heads down a hallway to the left of us, past the bar, and keeps walking, never turning around to see if I'm following her. I race to catch up and stop beside her when she pauses in front of a door labeled *Office*. Without bothering to knock, she opens the door to reveal a midsized office. In the center sits a middle-aged man with glasses hunched over his mahogany desk studying a slew of papers scattered on top of it. He looks up as we enter and sighs once he spots the girl in front of me.

"Sherry, how many times have I told you to knock?"

She smacks her gum loudly between her teeth and shrugs. "I dunno. A few."

He shakes his head in exasperation. "Right, well maybe try to knock next time, please?" Based on the frustration in his voice, this clearly isn't the first time they've had this conversation.

Sherry just shrugs in indifference. "Sure, whatever. Your interview is here."

She steps aside, and he finally seems to notice me standing there. He quickly scrambles as he stands up, sending a few papers on his desk flying to the ground, and straightens up his outfit by smoothing a hand down his shirt.

"Hello there. You must be Tatum," he says, sticking his hand out for me to shake and I walk forward to take it.

"That's me."

"OMG, wait." Sherry interjects, eyeing me. "Are you the new girl everyone's talking about?"

She says it so unabashedly that I feel my cheeks heat. "Uh, I guess so," I reply.

Mark scolds her, "Sherry!"

She holds up her hands to him in a pacifying way but looks at me up and down unapologetically. I tense up slightly, knowing that this might happen, but Sherry's face reveals nothing about what she thinks of me. We stare at each other a beat before she cracks a smile. I relax and return her smile, as if we're sharing some secret, when Mark clears his throat.

"If you don't mind, I have an interview to conduct here. Would you please close the door on your way out." He raises a pointed brow at Sherry, who rolls her eyes and mock salutes him as she turns to leave.

She turns and pauses next to me, leaning over to whisper, "It's so fun to mess with him," then shoots a wink in my way before walking out without closing the door. I stand there, staring after her, as Mark huffs and rounds his desk, shutting the door. It clicks into place and he gestures for me to take a seat across from him. I sit down and lean back into the chair, suddenly not that nervous for this interview anymore.

"So, have you ever worked in the food industry before?"

The interview lasted a total of five minutes, and I got the job with no problem, despite never having a job before. Although I have a sneaking suspicion it has more to do with Mark wanting to hire someone so Sherry doesn't keep bothering him than it does with my qualifications. I spent the next few hours shadowing Sherry and starting my training. At one point, I called Mary to ask if she could watch Emma for longer than expected since I was asked to work through the dinner shift. Getting Emma into daycare is the next thing on my to-do list because I don't want to keep relying on Mary.

As I'm planning this, I see Sherry approaching me now that the dinner rush has finally calmed down a bit. "How's it goin', new girl?" she says as she leans against the counter.

"Good. I think I've finally got the hang of it for the most part."

"You're a quick learner. It's mostly locals that come in here, especially this time of year, so you shouldn't have much trouble."

"Cool," I reply as an awkward silence descends over us.

"God, I can't wait to leave," she groans, stretching her back. We're huddled by the bar waiting for Mark to tell us our shift is over. "And who is that?" she drawls.

I turn to see who she's talking about and spot Chase wandering in, his eyes scanning the restaurant. A smile forms on my face, and I take a moment to get a good look at him. His dark wash jeans complement the white shirt he's wearing, even if they do have smears of black oil on them. I raise my hand to wave at him, but suddenly feel a tug on my arm, pulling it back down.

Sherry hisses in my ear. "What are you doing?!" I turn to her, completely confused at what she means. She rolls her eyes and explains. "You can't just wave a hot person over. You need to get them to come to you."

I laugh at her reasoning, but then realize she has no idea that's Chase. Which would make sense because until I introduced myself, she had no idea what I looked like either. She stares at me like I've grown two heads, and I clarify, "No, it's fine. That's just Chase."

"No way. *The* Chase?" she asks in amazement.

"The one and only."

She whistles, "Holy shit, girl. You got yourself one fine baby-daddy."

A flush creeps its way up my neck. I go to correct her but stop myself. We've always been quick to point out that Chase isn't Emma's father, but something holds me back this time. Maybe it's because after spending this time with him, I almost wish he were Emma's father. He's treated her with nothing but kindness, and it warms my heart when I see him taking care of her. So, I decide to keep my mouth shut and say nothing.

Sherry fans herself as she watches Chase make his way over to us. "I'd be jealous if I didn't see the way he looks at you."

I furrow my brows, wanting to ask her what she means by that, but Chase is already approaching us. As he gets closer, I realize Sherry might be right. He's looking at me with such affection, as if he's waited all day just until he can see me again. He jerks his chin to greet Sherry and smiles down at me. "Hey," he says, a twinkle in his eyes.

I smile back, feeling the flush return to my cheeks. "Hi."

"Oookay. I'm just going to go over here and fold something," Sherry says with a teasing note in her voice.

She gives me a look I can't quite decipher before walking towards Mark's office. I smile in the direction she disappeared, knowing she's likely bugging Mark about something.

"Who was that?" he nods to where Sherry has disappeared.

"That would be Sherry."

"Interesting."

"That she is." I tilt my head and look up at him. "Did you know we're practically famous here?"

He looks back down at me, giving me his full attention, and it steals my breath for a second. "Is that so?" A smirk forms at the corner of his mouth.

"Oh yeah. We're *the* Chase and Tatum, apparently."

"Well now that just sounds fun."

I go to reply right as I hear Sherry call out my name. "I'd better go see what she needs." I point to where she's waving me over. "You okay waiting a bit?"

"Yeah, no problem."

He takes an empty seat at the bar as I head to the back room. At that moment, I realize the way I've been feeling lately is impossible to deny any longer. I thought these feelings I had toward him were because we were forced into this situation together. Then I saw the way he was with Emma. And now, with the way I get butterflies every time I'm around him, I know it's more than that. I like him; *really* like him. I shake out my arms as I near the office and glance back at Chase one last time. He's sitting on the stool, watching me, and when our eyes meet, he gives me a slow smile. *Tonight*, I decide. Tonight, I'll tell him how I feel and lay it all out there.

CHAPTER 13

The drive home is quiet, and I'm lost in my thoughts as we pull into the driveway at Mary's house. It's already dark out, but all the lights inside the house are on, illuminating the front yard and casting shadows over it. Chase and I walk in silence towards the house and when we step inside, we find Mary and Conrad cuddled up on the couch, watching some wildlife program.

Mary spots us first and pauses their show. "How was it?" she asks.

"It was good," I reply with a long sigh. "Tiring, but good."

"I knew you'd get the job, kiddo," Conrad says as he stands up and walks over to us, pulling me in for a hug.

"Uh-huh. It couldn't have had anything to do with Sherry leaving, could it?" I say sarcastically.

Conrad just smiles at me as Mary waves a hand in the air and walks over. "Nonsense. Are you kids hungry? I have some chili in the fridge."

Without waiting for an answer, she heads over to the kitchen, Chase and Conrad trailing behind her. I'm slow to follow, my eyes fixating on the baby monitor on the coffee table. On the screen is the grainy image of Emma's sleeping form.

"No thanks," I tell her distractedly, my eyes still glued to the screen. "I already ate at work."

"She went down about thirty minutes ago." I jump, Mary's voice startling me. When I turn around, I see her poking her head out of the kitchen doorway, a hesitant smile on her face. "I wasn't sure what time you would be home. I know you probably wanted to put her to bed, but she started getting a little fussy."

I shake my head. "No, that's okay. Thank you for watching her."

"Anytime, sweetie. You know we don't mind."

"It's been a while since we've had a baby in the house." Conrad chuckles, but the sound quickly fades when he notices Mary shifting uncomfortably. I knit my brows together, wondering what the story is there.

Mary clasps her hands together, distracting us from the brief tension swirling around the room. "Well, I know it's been a long day for you two. Why don't you grab Emma and get some rest? I'll have breakfast ready in the morning if you'd like some."

"That'd be great, thanks. We still haven't gone grocery shopping," Chase chimes in.

Mary waves us off. "Well, that's what we're here for."

Chase gathers up Emma's loose belongings while I go into the room where her crib is. I pick her up as gently as I can so as not to wake her. We whisper our goodnights to Mary and Conrad, and then Chase and I make the short trek to our little home.

"Did she wake up at all?" Chase asks me after I've tucked Emma into her crib and joined him the kitchen.

"No. I thought she was about to at one point, but I think she was just dreaming," I reply, leaning my hip against the counter.

The silence that encompassed us back in the car is in full force as I wordlessly fiddle with my hands. I had promised myself that I would admit my feelings to him tonight, but the longer the silence stretches on, the more anxious I get. Without really thinking it through, I open my mouth, but nothing comes out. I clear my throat and try again.

"Chase, I—" My words are cut off when I hear a phone ding beside us.

Chase gives me an apologetic look and grabs his phone out of his pocket, the glow from the screen illuminating his face. He keeps his expression neutral as he reads the message, giving no indication of who it might be. After several beats, he locks the phone without replying and sets it on the counter.

"Who was that?" I ask, trying to sound as nonchalant as possible.

He shifts his weight ever so slightly, a tell that he's uncomfortable. "Just one of the waitresses at Flamingo's."

"Oh." I blink and am genuinely shocked by that answer.

He clears his throat. "Her name was Jenelle, I think. She, uh, came up to me when I was at the bar waiting for you and asked for my number." He squints down at the phone like he's offended at it.

"Oh," I repeat, "and you gave it to her?"

"Sort of," he says slowly, his eyes searching my face for a reaction.

I swallow down the lump forming in my throat. "What did she say?"

He narrows his eyes slightly at me. "She wanted to see if I was free Friday night."

"Like a date?"

"I guess, yeah," he shrugs disinterestedly.

My heart sinks the longer this conversation goes on, and I force myself to ask the one question I really don't want to know the answer to. "Are you going to go?"

He studies me closely for a beat before responding. "I don't think so."

Feeling frustrated, I roughly blurt, "You should go."

He raises his eyebrows, the only indication of surprise from my response on his otherwise neutral face. "I should?" he asks slowly.

I nod as I start to back away, wanting to get out of here as fast as possible, already feeling the tears welling up behind my eyes. "Yeah, I mean, why not, right?" I can feel him staring at me, but I can't bring myself to look at him. Instead, I keep my eyes on the floor in front of me. "I'm going to head to bed. It's, uh, been a long day—starting the new job and everything." I turn quickly and start walking down the hallway, not waiting for a response.

"Tatum."

He calls out just as I reach my room, and my hand pauses over the doorknob. I really don't want to turn around, but it's like my body has a mind of its own, looking back against my will. He's standing at the opening of the hallway, staring at me. It seems like he wants to say more, but I can tell there's an internal debate going on inside his head. I hold my breath, waiting to see if he'll say anything else. Finally, he opens his mouth and for a moment I think I'll get something more, before he snaps it closed just as quickly. When his shoulders deflate, I know I'll never know what he really wanted to say.

"Goodnight, Tatum," he says softly.

I smile sadly back at him. "Night, Chase."

I turn and quickly rush into my room. As soon as the door is shut behind me, I lean up against it and bang my head on it, letting out a frustrated groan.

I decide to skip out on breakfast at Mary's and go to the daycare early the next morning. There are only a few cars in the parking lot when I get there. I borrowed Mary's car since Chase will be taking his to work. Not that we've talked since that upsetting conversation last night. At least by coming here and getting this taken care of as soon as possible, I can avoid any thoughts about

Chase and how he clearly doesn't feel the same way about me. I unload Emma from the backseat and walk to the front door. The daycare looks like it's upgraded from its previous spot in Mary's realtor office space. This is probably twice the size and located a little bit farther out of town, nestled by the cliffside. I expect to hear a range of screaming kids when I walk in, but instead, it's peacefully quiet.

"Hi there. Can I help you?"

I look to my right and see a middle-aged woman sitting behind the front desk. Like Mary's office, there's a large mural on the wall behind her. Instead of sea life, though, this one is a blue wall with white fluffy clouds and a sun in the corner.

"Um, yeah," I say while adjusting Emma's car seat to my other arm and walking over to the desk. "My name's Tatum, and I was wondering if I could get my daughter, Emma, in here for daycare?"

"Sure, let me see what we can do. How old is she?"

"Five months."

The woman gives me a warm smile. "Well, we should have plenty of room in Mrs. Clark's class, but let me check to make sure."

"Yeah, of course. Thank you." I wait patiently as she types on the keyboard.

"Okay, it looks like you should be all set," she says. After a few more clicks on the computer, the printer behind her whirls to life, spitting out a page filled with prices. "Here's a list of the different rates we offer. I'll call Mrs. Clark's room to let her know we'll be stopping by."

"Okay. Thank you."

She picks up the phone, and as I hear her talking to Mrs. Clark, I look around the room again. On one of the walls is a collage of pictures of different children all smiling and looking happy.

"If you'll follow me, we can head on back," she says, sliding out from behind the desk.

I follow her through the stained-glass door on the left. As we continue walking down the hallway, she turns her head to talk to me. "The kids have different nap schedules, depending on how old they are and what classroom they're in. Sometimes the naps overlap, which is why it's currently as quiet as it is."

"Oh," I say as we stop abruptly in front of a door decorated with paper cutouts of apples, each with different names in the middle.

"And here we are."

She knocks on the door and a younger woman opens it up. She smiles when she sees us and waves us into the room. "Hi there, I'm Mrs. Clark. And you must be—" The question fades as she waits for me to introduce myself.

"Tatum," I say, extending my free hand out for her to shake. "And this is Emma." I lift the car seat up a tad, where Emma's watching us intently.

"Welcome to our classroom," she smiles proudly. "It's nice to meet you."

"Thank you, it's nice to meet you too." I glance around the room and notice several cribs along the wall and three other babies in their swings.

We talk for a bit longer before the receptionist, whose name I learned was Sandra, walks me around the rest of the daycare. She tells me about the kids' other teachers and the different age groups they have. It ranges from a few months old to kindergarten. Emma would have those three other babies I saw in the classroom with her. Mrs. Clark said she also usually has an assistant in the classroom with her, but she was out sick for the day.

They never once ask about Emma's dad, which makes me like them, and this place, even more. After we finish the tour, I sign Emma up for a six-week trial period to see how well she does here. As I'm filling out all the forms, I hesitate at the section listing emergency contacts. In the end, I decide to put Chase's name down. Even if things are currently a little weird between us, he's been there for Emma, and I know he will continue to be.

I know I'm cutting it close to Emma's nap time when I leave with how fussing she's getting. When we get back to the cottage, I give Emma a bottle before changing her diaper and settling her down in her crib for a nap. As soon as I put her down, she immediately falls asleep. With the monitor in hand, I head back to the couch and decide to lie down for a little bit. I can feel my eyes starting to get heavy, so I close them—just for a minute.

I wake up suddenly, disoriented, and look around, trying to figure out what woke me up. It must be mid-afternoon now, given how much shadier it's gotten in the cottage. Other than that, I don't see anything out of the ordinary. I reach over to turn on the lamp on the side table and as I do, a blanket slips from my lap onto the ground. I stare down at it in confused because I know I didn't have it over me when I fell asleep. In fact, it wasn't anywhere near me; we keep it in a basket next to the TV across the room, so I know I didn't get it myself. Mary has a key, but I highly doubt she'd let herself in like that.

Sighing, I get up to check on Emma. I open the door to my room, and my stomach drops when I see Emma's crib is empty. I frantically look around for her and run back into the living room. My eye catches on a note next to her monitor.

Emma woke up and I took her up to Mary's house so you could get a little more sleep. Thought you might need it. - Chase.

That must've been what woke me up—Chase leaving the cottage. I let out a sigh of relief and sink down onto the couch, letting my heart rate return to normal. That means he put that blanket over me, too. I'm not sure how I should take that, so I tell the butterflies in my stomach to settle down at his kind gesture. Not wanting to dwell on it any longer, I head up to Mary's house. I'm not sure where Chase has gone to, but when I get there, I find Mary is playing with Emma on a playmat, her toys scattered all around. I appreciate Chase doing that for me, and I wish he was still around so I could thank him in person.

The next day I go to work and am instantly dreading it. It's not because I don't want to work, but because today is Friday—the night Chase is going on his date. I left Emma with Mary and Conrad instead of taking her to daycare since I'm working a double shift today. It's my last shift training with Sherry, and I hate to admit it, but I'll miss working with her. We go through our training routine throughout the day, but it's just after seven when my night gets significantly worse. I have just finished seating an older couple when I see Chase stroll in through the door. His hair has that messy look going on, as though he's run his fingers through it a thousand times. He's wearing a loose shirt over his jeans and a pair of white sneakers. He looks casual while still somehow looking incredible. I watch as a girl in a yellow flower sundress comes flouncing up to him. Her black hair is slicked back into a high ponytail, and I immediately recognize her as one of the waitresses who works here. Which means that must be Jenelle.

Then, to my horror, I watch as they sit down at one of the tables in the corner on the patio. My stomach churns, and I force myself to walk back to the hostess stand. I try to ignore their presence as I seat people throughout the evening, and it takes everything in me not to keep glancing over at them. Which is difficult to do because I hear her high-pitched laugh about every five seconds. It felt like it took forever to get him to be that carefree with me and the fact that he's making her laugh so easily makes me want to cry.

Finally, after what feels like an eternity, I see them get up from the table. Like a coward, I hide in the corner by the office so they won't see me. Chase quickly scans the room as he's leaving, and my traitorous heart wants to believe he's looking for me.

Sherry comes up to me in my hiding spot, watching as they walk out the door. "Uh, what was that?"

I cut my eyes to her. "What do you mean?"

She looks at me like I've suddenly grown two heads. "The two of them together."

"They're on a date," I explain, shrugging.

"I can see that," she says, rolling her eyes at me. "What I mean is *what was that*. Don't you two have a baby together?"

I groan, shaking my head. "I told him to go. We're not together; he can date if he wants to."

She arches her perfectly shaped brow at me. "Since when?"

I straighten. "What are you talking about?"

"Since when are you two not together? Because it sure looked like it the other night."

"Yeah, well, we're not. I mean, I thought there might have been something there, but then he gave his number to Jenelle, and I'm not about to confess my feelings to him if he doesn't feel the same way."

She shakes her head. "Look, I know we don't really know each other, but I think there's something there. It would be a shame to waste it just because you're scared."

I cross my arms over my chest defensively. "I'm not scared. I'm just being realistic. I have Emma to worry about, and I don't want to make things awkward between the two of us."

She holds her hands up. "I'm not trying to butt in; I'm just telling you what I see. Do what you want with that."

"I'll think about it ..."

"Okay," she concedes, nudging my arm. "Come on, let's get back to work."

I'm quiet for the rest of my shift and I'm more than ready to go home by the time it's over. When I get to Mary's house, I get Emma from her with a quick thank you before heading to the cottage. I'm sure she notices my sour mood, but thankfully doesn't comment. I lay Emma down in her crib and then climb into bed. For some reason, I choose to torment myself further by lying awake in bed, listening for Chase to get home. It's hard to stop my mind from wandering off with images of him and Jenelle cozied up on her couch or going for late night walks on the beach. Jealousy rears its ugly head, making me even more frustrated with this entire situation. Finally, the front door opens and closes just before midnight. I hear his heavy footsteps briefly stop outside my door before continuing to his room. I groan and roll over in bed, letting sleep consume me.

Chase is gone when I wake up the next morning and seems to make himself scarce the rest of the day. Even after I come home from taking Emma shopping, his door is closed, and the lights are off.

Sunday morning rolls around and I get ready for another double shift at Flamingo's. I pack Emma's bag with her things and hoist her in my arms, making our way to Mary's house to drop her off for the day. When we get there, I'm surprised to see Chase in the kitchen wearing his work overalls, a plate of eggs and bacon in front of him.

"Hey," I say awkwardly.

He looks up at me briefly before casting his eyes downward. "Hey."

Conrad's standing there watching our stilted conversation with a bemused expression. Mary comes into the kitchen just then and notices our stiff postures. She chuckles lightly, saying, "Well, good morning, everyone."

"Morning," I mumble. "Are you sure you're okay with watching Emma for the day?" I ask Mary.

Conrad waves me off before she can reply, though. "You know we don't mind, kiddo."

"What time do you have to be at work?" Mary asks.

Her question saves me from my own uneasiness, and I glance over at the clock. "In about fifteen minutes."

She nods and walks over to the kitchen island, putting an already made sandwich into a bag. "Here," she says, handing the sandwich to me. "You can eat it on your break."

"Thank you."

She then turns her attention to Chase. "I heard you had quite the eventful Friday night."

He looks up from his plate and mutters, "I wouldn't call it eventful."

"What would you call it then?" I blurt. Everyone looks at me and I instantly feel my cheeks heat.

Chase tilts his head to one side and then shrugs. "It was okay. Won't be happening again though."

"Oh dear, why not?" Mary asks as I bite my tongue.

Chase gives me a fleeting glance before he turns his attention back to Mary. "I'm just not really interested in dating anyone right now."

"Well, that's too bad. She's a lovely girl."

I narrow my eyes at her, the traitor. She turns her attention to me with a grin playing on her lips, and I school my features. "That reminds me. I spoke to Quinn the other day and she mentioned that her son would be in town for the weekend. I thought about how nice it would be if the two of you could get together."

I narrow my eyes at her, wondering who the heck Quinn is and why I would want to meet her son. I glance over at Chase and find him white knuckling the fork in his hand. He's glaring down at his food but doesn't make a move to eat any of it. I look up in time to see Mary wink so quickly I almost miss it.

"I have to go to work," Chase announces suddenly, an edge to his voice that wasn't there before, and pushes back from the table, his chair scraping against the floor.

Mary looks over at Conrad with a mischievous glint in her eyes and he smiles at her. "Chase, would you mind taking Tatum to work? We were going to take Emma to the park."

"Oh, you don't –"

"Sure," he interrupts my protests, putting his plate in the sink and turning to me. "You about ready?"

"Um, yeah." I shoot a final glance in Mary's direction who is suspiciously avoiding my stare.

I bend down to give Emma a kiss goodbye before following him out the front door. We get in the car and there's an uncomfortable silence between us.

"So …" I say, breaking the tension. As casual as possible, I ask, "Are you going to see Jenelle again?"

He shakes his head without looking at me. "Definitely not."

I stop picking at my nails and look at him. "But I thought that you've been hanging out with her?"

He finally looks at me, confusion clouding his features. "What makes you think that?" he asks suspiciously.

"Uh, the fact that you've been practically MIA since you had that date with her," I state.

He shakes his head in annoyance. "Trust me, I haven't been with her." That isn't the answer I was expecting. I'm about to ask where he's been then when he suddenly jerks the car to a stop. "We're here."

I look up and see that we're in front of the restaurant. I guess I was too preoccupied by our conversation to notice how fast we got here. I turn to face him. "Chase, I—" I start, but stop myself when he glances over at me. He just shakes his head and smiles miserably.

"I'll pick you up after your shift," he says sadly.

"Okay," I whisper, more confused than I was before.

I get out of the car in a daze. He waits until I walk inside before driving off. I slip into my usual routine at work, praying to the stars above that Jenelle isn't working tonight. I believe Chase when he admitted he wasn't with her, but I also don't want to hear her talk about him and any stories she may tell. Thankfully, my wishes are granted when I go through my shift without a glimpse of Jenelle. Although, my thoughts are still a little preoccupied with Chase throughout the evening. There's so much I want to know, while also being afraid of hearing it. One thing that I know for sure is that I don't want to live in this state of limbo anymore.

CHAPTER 14

The night passes in a blur, and by the time Chase picks me up for the night, I'm feeling exhausted. I know Emma's already asleep at Mary's, and I hate the thought of waking her up to take her home, but I haven't fully come around to having her spend the night there yet. She's only ever stayed with me, and I know it will be hard for me when she eventually does.

I head to Mary's house to get Emma while Chase goes in the opposite direction to our cottage. After I pick her up from Mary's, I walk back to our cottage. When I walk in, I spot Chase bent over the stove. He doesn't say anything, so I head straight to my room. Emma barely stirs as I lay her down in her crib, so I grab the monitor and walk back out into the kitchen.

"What are you doing?" I ask when I notice cream and chocolate on the counter next to him.

"Making hot chocolate. Want some?"

"Sure." I walk over and lean up against the counter next to him, watching him work.

"My mom used to make this all the time. She hated using the powder mix, said the flavor just wasn't the same, so she showed me how to make it from scratch."

"Sounds yummy."

He smiles over at me. "It is. Somehow, she always knew whenever I was feeling down or upset as a kid and would make this for me. It never failed to make me feel better."

"Mom's intuition." I hesitate with what I want to say, not sure how he might take it, but decide to say it anyway. "I wish I could've met her."

His hand freezes, halting his stirring, before he resumes and looks over at me. "She would've liked you."

A warmth spreads through my chest at his admission and I smile. "Anything I can help with?" I ask, changing the subject.

"Actually yeah, come here." He beckons me over to stand in front of the stove. "Can you stir the cream?"

I nod and do as he says, stirring the cream with the wooden spoon. He comes up behind me and grabs my hand, guiding us to stir the cream together. "The key is to keep stirring it like this, so the cream doesn't get overheated," he explains. I nod, but I'm distracted by how close he's standing behind me. After a few seconds of stirring, he clears his throat and backs away, and I instantly feel the loss of his warmth. "Yeah, uh, just like that. I'll get started on the chocolate."

"Okay," I whisper, barely able to find my voice. We work silently next to one another, and I steal a few glances to watch him cut up the bar of chocolate.

"Just keep stirring it while I put the chocolate in." I watch as the chocolate slowly melts into the cream, filling the air with a delicious aroma. I keep stirring until the last bit of chocolate has disappeared. Chase pulls two mugs down from the cabinet and grabs the ladle on the counter to scoop the hot chocolate into both mugs.

"Thank you," I say when he hands me my mug. I follow him into the living room and we sit down on the couch next to each other, sipping our hot chocolate silently, both lost in our own thoughts tonight.

"Why are you upset tonight?" I ask, breaking the silence with a question that's been plaguing my mind ever since he mentioned it earlier.

"What?"

"Earlier you said your mom used to make this for you when you felt down or upset. So why are you upset tonight?"

He lets out a deep sigh, staring into his empty mug before setting it down on the coffee table. Leaning back into the couch, he tilts his head and focuses on a spot on the wall in front of us. "A lot of things, I guess."

"Care to elaborate?"

A ghost of a smile graces his lips before it's gone. He turns to face me. "Do you ever feel like there's two distinct paths you can take, but you're not entirely sure which one is the best for you?"

I stare at him, confused at what he's talking about. "What do you mean?"

He shakes his head. "Never mind."

"No, don't do that." I let out an exasperated groan. "I thought we were past all this. I thought we had gotten closer, yet ever since we've been here, you've been distant with me. What's going on?"

"I know, and that's exactly what I'm talking about."

I throw my hands up in frustration. "That doesn't make any sense."

"Yes, it does, Tatum. Just think about it."

"What, are you trying to decide if you want to be with Jenelle or something? Are you saying I'm in the way of that?"

"Jesus, it has absolutely nothing to do with her!"

"Okay, then what is it? Because I'm honestly so confused right now."

"It's you!" he shouts suddenly. "I want to be with you."

We stare at each other, wide-eyed and stunned into silence in the aftermath of his confession. He lets out a breath and I hold my index finger up before he tries to say anything else.

"Okay," I say slowly. "Just to be clear, you want to be with me because you feel like you have this obligation to stay until Emma and I are settled, or do you want to be with me because—"

"Because I'm in love you." He lets out a sarcastic laugh. "I don't want to leave you because I can't imagine not knowing what you and Emma are doing—what your day looks like. Because I hate the thought of not seeing Emma take her first steps or the idea of another guy taking you on a date."

He smiles softly and looks at me carefully. "I don't want to know what it's like not to hear your laugh or listen to your quirky jokes; not to see the blush on your face or watch you be the incredible mom that you are. As much as it terrifies me to admit all of this to you, knowing what I might miss out on terrifies me more."

"But then why did you go on a date with Jenelle?" I shake my head, still not understanding.

He huffs out a humorless laugh. "I only went because you told me to."

I shake my head again, trying to process this. "That's because I thought you liked her. That's why you gave her your phone number."

"No," he says, shaking his head vehemently. "Not intentionally. I mean technically, yes, she did get my number, but that's only because she grabbed my phone out of my hand when I was waiting for you. She texted herself before I had a chance to stop her. I never intended to respond to her, but when you told me to go, I thought I misread this whole situation with us."

I put my head in both hands, shaking it back and forth and laugh at the irony of this all. I look up and see the confusion on his face. "What?" he asks.

"I was going to tell you how I felt that night. I worked up the courage to finally tell you that *I'm* in love with *you*, but then she texted you. I got so upset because I thought you liked her that I just wanted to leave so that's why I told you go."

"You're in love with me?" His eyes light up with excitement as a smile spreads across his face, ignoring everything else I said. I nod, unable to form words, not fully believing that this is real.

He leans closer and takes my hand in his, locking them together. I look down at our intertwined hands and suddenly blurt, "I've had a crush on you since I first met you."

He leans back and raises an eyebrow. "Seriously?"

I nod with a smile. "Yup. Ever since you cannonballed into the pool." He shakes his head with a laugh. "What?" I ask, confused.

"Nothing, it's just that I kind of had a crush on you that summer, too."

I stare at him, surprised. "You did?"

"I did. I liked that you were a little shy, with your gap tooth and pigtails." He reaches out and flicks the ends of my brown hair.

I roll my eyes. "I only wore my hair like that twice."

He shrugs. "Yeah, but I remember."

He leans closer until he's right in front of me, just inches away from my face, and I hold my breath in anticipation. "You're sure?" he whispers softly, his scent surrounding me. I'm not exactly sure what question he's asking, but I know there's no turning back at this point. I do the only thing I want to do and nod my head.

"I'm very sure."

He smiles slowly and then leans in the rest of the way, his lips gingerly touching mine. It's an unhurried kiss at first and I savor the way he tastes; the hot chocolate still lingering on his lips. I don't hesitate as I lean in, kissing him with urgency. He swipes his tongue over my lips, asking for entrance, and I open my mouth for him. Our tongues clash together as he threads a hand through my hair at the base of my neck. The butterflies take full flight in my stomach and fireworks ignite behind my closed eyes, loving the feel of his lips on mine. After what feels like a lifetime of kissing him, he pulls away with one final gentle kiss on my lips. He leans back slightly and watches my reaction, his eyes bouncing back and forth. I'm helpless to stop the smile that spreads across my face and without thinking about it, I lean forward to kiss him one more time, not wanting this moment to end.

"So," I say when I pull back, "is this why you've been MIA this weekend?"

He laughs loudly. "Something like that. It was hard being around you when all I wanted to do was kiss you." He gently brushes his lips across mine to emphasize his point.

I groan when he pulls away. "How do you think I felt? I got so jealous when I saw you with Jenelle." He leans back into the couch, and I curl up against him, my head resting on his chest. "What does this mean for us now?"

He gives a one shoulder shrug. "Well, we've skipped the whole getting to know one another part I guess, but I would like to take you out on a date."

I feel giddy at that idea, more than I've ever felt in my entire life. "I'd really like that."

"Good."

We sit in comfortable silence for a few minutes before I glance up at him, my chin on his chest. "I know we should probably go to bed, but I'm wide awake right now," I whisper softly.

He looks back down at me. "Me too," he whispers back. "Here." He pulls the blanket down from the back of the couch and wraps it around us. "You good?"

I smile. "I'm perfect."

"Yes, you are." A blush works its way up, making cheeks feel like they're on fire. He swipes his thumb over the spot. "I love it when you blush."

I feel my cheeks darken to a deep maroon and hide my face in his chest, not used to these compliments coming from him. He laughs at me but doesn't say anything. He wraps his arms around me and kisses the top of my head. "Goodnight, Tatum."

"Night, Chase."

With a contented sigh, I relax into his arms. His breathing evens out as he drifts off to sleep and I snuggle closer to him, enjoying the feeling of his arms around me. I don't know what the future will look like, but I know that right now I've never felt this happy.

~

I groggily peel my eyes open to the sunlight drifting in. My back is incredibly stiff, and I try to sit up, but an arm is draped over me. I glance up and find Chase sleeping, his arms wrapped tightly around me. We're still in the same position we fell asleep in, so I gently peel his arms off me. He stirs when I stretch my arms above my head and mumbles a good morning.

"Good morning to you too," I say.

He leans forward and kisses me, making me realize last night wasn't a dream. Happiness explodes inside me, and I climb into his lap, straddling him, the blanket tangling around us. His arms wrap around me, holding me tightly, his fingers splayed across my back. I'm so caught up in the kiss that it takes me a moment to remember I haven't brushed my teeth yet. I pull back quickly and cover my mouth with my hand.

"I probably have awful morning breath," I admit shyly.

He shrugs. "If you do, then I'm used to it. You do remember that we were on the road together, staying in all those rundown motels, right?"

I slap his arm. "Yeah, but that was before we were, you know," I gesture between us, "this."

He shakes his head. "I didn't care then, and I don't care now."

He leans in again and gives me a long, slow kiss. I melt into him and grip the collar of his shirt, needing him like I need my next breath. He pulls back and I groan. He chuckles and tucks a piece of my hair behind my ear.

"We probably need to check on Emma."

I sigh. "Right."

I untangle myself from blanket and stand up, stretching out my limbs one more time. I walk towards my room, Chase following closely behind me. I turn and call out over my shoulder, "You know, I could get used to that."

"What, the kissing?" he smiles playfully.

"No, the *we* going to check on Emma part," I pause to think about it and add, "well, the kissing part too."

He slings his arm around my shoulders and kisses my hair. "Get used to it because I'm not going anywhere."

"Good." I smile at him.

We wake Emma up and start the morning routine of dressing, feeding, and changing her diaper. We work together seamlessly, and I enjoy his company rather than feeling like Emma and I are a burden. Once we've finished everything, I figure it's time to tackle one more thing that's been on my mind.

I bite my lip as I look at Chase. "We should probably call Courtney and update her about where we are. I'm sure she's been freaking out."

"Yeah, you're probably right. Why don't you call her now?"

I look at the clock and grab the burner phone from my purse. "She's in class right now."

He takes the phone from my hand and types something quickly before setting it down on the counter. Not even thirty seconds later I hear the shrill ringtone of an incoming call, and I look at Chase in amazement.

"What'd you text her?"

His lips curl up into a smirk. "SOS."

I roll my eyes and with a laugh answer the phone. "Hey—"

"What the hell is happening? Are you okay? Why'd you text SOS? Your parents didn't find you, did they? I mean, I thought they weren't looking for you, but did something happen?"

I pull the phone away from my ear and put it on speaker as

she rambles all that out in one breath, each question blending into the other. She takes a deep breath, and I know she's about to bombard me with more questions so I stop her before she can continue.

"Easy there, killer. We're all okay," I explain. I think back to all the questions she asked and try to answer them as fast as I can. "Chase and Emma are right here with me, and no, my parents didn't find us."

"Oh, thank God. Tatum Marie Rothchild, you had me worried sick. Why'd you text SOS? You had me freaking out!"

I roll my eyes. "Sorry, that was all Chase."

"What—"

"Hey sis," Chase smirks, even though she can't see him.

"And yes, we've settled down." I cut her off before she questions me further. "We found a really cute house we're renting from a lady who kind of took us under her wing. She got me a new ID and everything."

"That's amazing. Now tell me everything," she says right as I hear a bell come through the speaker.

"Where are you?"

"Girl's bathroom. As soon as I saw your text I ran out of the class to call you."

"I guess we don't have much time to talk then, but you can call me when get home and we can talk more, okay?"

"Yeah, okay," she sighs. "I have Mrs. Hensworth right now, and you know how mean she can be if you're late."

I blink back unexpected tears. "I remember. I really miss you, Court."

"I miss you too."

"Aw, miss you too, sis," Chase chimes in and I slap my hand against his arm for ruining the sentimental moment we were having. "Ouch."

"Wait," Courtney starts, "can you at least tell me where you are?"

I hesitate for a split second, just enough time for Chase to notice. Luckily, he jumps in and says, "Let's just say you may want to start applying to colleges in California."

"Seriously? That's all I get? You can't just leave me hanging like that!" She whines.

"I know, I know. I'm sorry. We'll talk more about it later, okay? But we're settled, and we both have jobs in town."

"We? You're staying there too, Chase?" He looks over at me with the question in his eyes. I nod, knowing this will be a bombshell we're about to drop on her.

"I am," he says slowly, his eyes glued to mine. "I'm going to be staying with Tatum and Emma for a while."

"We're, um, kind of dating?" It comes out more of a question and I look at Chase for clarification. It may be forward of me, but I'm not sure what else to call it.

"We are," he assures me, and a grin spreads across my face.

"You're what!?" she screeches down the line.

I wince. "It's new and just sort of happened," I explain. "But yeah, we're together."

It's quiet on the line and I nibble my lip between my teeth, worried that she might be upset that we're together. Instead, there's a loud squeal.

"I freaking knew it!"

There's muffled noises coming through the phone, and I can just picture her doing a little happy dance right there in the girl's bathroom.

"Seriously?" I ask.

"Well duh. I knew it was only a matter of time."

"You did not," I argue.

"Uh-huh. I could tell it would happen as soon as you two laid eyes on each other."

I shake my head. "Whatever. You do need to get back to class before you get in trouble and we need to eat before Chase has to go to work."

She sniffles, fake crying, "They grow up so fast."

I roll my eyes again. "Bye, you weirdo."

"I'll call you when I get home."

"Love you, Court."

"Love you too, mama."

We hang up and I feel ten times lighter. I didn't realize how much I needed to talk to her. I wish I would've called her sooner and talked to her about my feelings for Chase because she would've known exactly what to say.

"It was good to talk to her," Chase muses.

I lean into him and smile contentedly. "Yeah, it was."

"Come on, want to go tell Mary and Conrad?" he says teasingly.

I giggle and he holds out his hand to me. I slip mine into his, intertwining our fingers together. With Emma in his arms, we walk hand in hand up to the house. The smell of bacon greets us as we walk in, and I see Mary by the stove cooking breakfast while Conrad's sitting at the table reading the newspaper. They both look up when they hear us come in, and it's almost comical how their eyes immediately go to our locked hands. Mary drops her spatula and starts clapping excitedly.

"Oh, it's about time," she exclaims and comes over to wrap us all in a big hug.

"Mary, let them breathe. You're embarrassing them," Conrad says, shaking his head.

"It's fine." I wave him off because, deep down, I enjoy the amount of time she spends gushing over us.

"Come, sit. Do you want to stay for breakfast? I'm just finishing up." We nod and take our usual spots around the table as Mary piles our plates with food. Once she joins us with her own plate, we all dig in.

"Now, do we need to have the talk?" She says half-jokingly, but I can sense there's a serious undertone.

I huff out a laugh. "I already have a baby; I think we're past the point of 'the talk'."

Mary shakes her head. "Which is precisely my point. We don't want another baby running around here so soon, now do we?"

Chase chokes on his orange juice, spitting some of it back into his cup. I stare at Mary in wide-eyed mortification, a blush flushing my cheeks bright red, embarrassed that she wants to have this conversation now, especially in front of Chase and Conrad.

Conrad levels his wife with a stern look. "Now, Mary, they don't need us butting in. They're old enough."

"You're right," she replies, giving him a meaningful look then directing her attention to us. "I'm sorry. We're not your parents; we shouldn't be telling you what to do."

"It's okay," Chase and I say in unison.

Then I look back and forth between the two of them, noticing how tense they are. "What's going on?" I ask.

Conrad looks at me and smiles, patting my hand on the table reassuringly. "Nothing you need to worry about."

"We had a son," Mary blurts suddenly.

"Mary," Conrad cautions gently.

"No, it's okay. I want to tell them." She takes a deep breath and continues. "We had a son not that much older than you, Chase. He had just turned twenty-one. He was home for the summer and went out one evening to meet up with some friends. It wasn't even that late at night, but another driver had too much to drink and wasn't paying attention to the road." She pauses to gather herself, tears glistening in her eyes. I feel my own start to get misty.

"He swerved into the other lane and hit Kyle head on. That was our son, Kyle. The other driver's car went over the cliff. They both died instantly. We were told Kyle didn't suffer, but it was still hard to come to terms with it for a while. We still struggle with it sometimes." I swipe at the tears falling down my cheeks now. She reaches out to grab my hand in hers and then does the same with Chase. "That's why when I met you two, I wanted to help. Something about you kids reminded me of Kyle and brought back the life in this house we didn't know we needed."

She gives us a bittersweet smile. "You two and Emma. That's why we love making food for you or watching Emma. It means more to us than you can know."

I look at Conrad and he's nodding in agreement with her, tears making their silent trek down his face. Chase and I glance at each other. He doesn't have to say it, but I know what he's thinking; Mary reminds him of his mom. And they remind me of the parents I never really had—kind, caring, and loving. Somehow, along the way, we formed a family created from each of our broken pieces, and we're learning to rebuild those pieces together. A smile overtakes my face as I realize I'm giving my daughter something she was so close to being denied—a family.

I look around the room through my tears, our hands still clasped in Mary's, and I think this is what happiness looks like. All the little moments we've created that have brought us to this point—sitting around a table with a family I never imagined I'd have. Chase's sparkling eyes meet mine once again, and I know this is exactly where I'm meant to be.

MEET THE AUTHOR

Savannah Reed was born and raised in Charleston, South Carolina and grew up spending time at the beach, horseback riding, and shopping down on King Street. She attended an arts school for dance in Charleston and went on to earn a BA in English from Clemson University. She currently resides in Chattanooga, Tennessee with her husband and their Catahoula Leopard Dog, Blue Belle. When she's not going on hikes in the mountains of Tennessee, you can find her at the beach with a good book, cheering on the Clemson Tigers, or enjoying movies with a big bowl of popcorn.

OTHER TITLES FROM

5 PRINCE PUBLISHING